A NIGHTINGALE
SANG IN
FERNHURST ROAD

A NIGHTINGALE SANG IN FERNHURST ROAD

A SCHOOLBOY'S JOURNAL OF 1945

CHRISTOPHER MATTHEW

JOHN MURRAY
ALBEMARLE STREET, LONDON

Illustrated
by
David Eccles

© Christopher Matthew 1998
Illustrations © David Eccles 1998

First published in 1998
by John Murray (Publishers) Ltd,
50 Albemarle Street, London W1X 4BD

A catalogue record for this book is available from the British
Library

ISBN 0–7195–5899 9

Typeset in Baskerville by Servis Filmsetting Ltd, Manchester
Printed and bound in Great Britain by
The University Press, Cambridge

FOR ALAN COREN

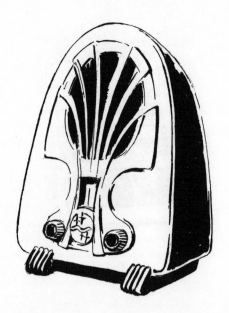

'Mr Churchill came on the wireless after lunch' (p. 13)

MAY

I WOKE up early, about half-past six. I went into Mummy's room but she wasn't there. I went downstairs and found her sitting at the table in the morning room.

She was drinking a cup of tea and listening to the wireless. She didn't say 'Good morning' or anything, she just looked at me. I thought for a moment she was going to cry but instead she said, 'Come over here, darling.' She put her arms round me and hugged me. Then she said, 'Hitler has committed suicide. They've just announced it on the news. The war's nearly over. That means Daddy will be coming home.'

I asked her how. She said, 'On a troopship, I expect.'

I said, 'What was Hitler doing on a troopship?'

She frowned and said she didn't know what I meant. I said that I wondered how Hitler had committed suicide. She said how should *she* know? He was dead, that was all that mattered. He probably took poison, knowing the sort of man he was.

Obviously she didn't actually know Hitler herself, but she's usually right, except when she tries to help me with my arithmetic homework. Last time she tried to help, I got three out of ten and I had to go and stand outside Chimp Harris's study all through Break. Everyone calls the headmaster Chimp. He looks exactly like something out of the Monkey House at the Zoo, especially when he scratches his chin.

In Chapel this morning he gave a long talk about guts and said that Hitler's problem was that he had no backbone. He said there is nothing more despicable in the eyes of God than a man who takes to the rugger field and is quite happy to shout instructions at others but won't get his own knees dirty.

Mr Churchill was not only a great captain and a great pack leader, but he was in the thick of the scrum from start to finish and got his man down every time. But when the going got tough and it really mattered, Hitler had funked the big tackle and the score at the final whistle would haunt him for eternity in the fires of hell.

Wednesday, May 2nd

I WAS out in the shed oiling the chain on my bike this evening after supper when Mummy came out and told me that the Germans had surrendered in Italy to Field Marshal Alexander.

I said, 'Does that mean the war is over?' She said, 'In Italy, yes.' I don't know why they don't give up everywhere.

Thursday, May 3rd

MUMMY woke me up this morning and said, 'Berlin has fallen.' I asked her if that was that. She said she wasn't sure but she hoped so. It's all very peculiar. What's the point in going on if you know you're going to be bashed up? I'd definitely give up if I were the Germans. I gave up when Gilbert said he was going to knock my teeth down my throat. But then everyone gives up when Gilbert's in one of his bashing-up moods.

We had rabbit in sick for lunch.

Friday, May 4th

WETHERBY-BROWN and I were clearing our table after lunch when The Chimp came in and said he had a special announcement to make. He said, 'It has just been reported on the BBC that the German forces in North-West Europe, Holland and Denmark have surrendered to Field Marshal Montgomery in his tent on Lüneburg Heath. It is only a matter of time now before we can start celebrating the end of the war. Meanwhile, may I remind you that the House Cricket-Ball-Throwing Competition starts at 2 p.m. promptly, not 2.15 as per the notice-board.'

I said to The Chimp that Monty's tent must be the biggest in the world. He asked me why and I said that the Cubs' tent which is quite big only takes twenty boys standing up plus Akela and Baloo, so a tent that's big enough for all those German forces to surrender in must be bigger than Wembley Stadium. The Chimp said, 'Is there insanity in your family, Bodge?' and smacked me hard round the side of the head and walked away. He always calls me Bodge. I wish he wouldn't.

In Latin today we learnt a new construction called the Accusative and Infinitive. It is used for reported speech. I asked Gnasher Davies if the BBC would have used the Accusative and Inifitive if Monty had been a Roman general and they had reported his speech. Gnasher said, 'I sometimes think you'll go to any lengths to get a laugh.'

Why do schoolmasters always assume we're trying to make fun of them?

Saturday, May 5th

IT was very hot this afternoon so Colin and I went down tothe stream at the bottom of Oakwood Meadow and collected frog-spawn in jam jars. Colin says that a small frog can lay between two and three thousand eggs in one go and a large one can lay as many as eight thousand. He read it in his *Wonder Book of Nature*.

I've put my spawn on the window ledge in the kitchen. It makes school tapioca look quite tasty.

Sunday, May 6th

THE wireless has been on all weekend waiting for news of the end of the war, but it still hasn't come.

Mummy said that it's only a matter of time and then Daddy will be on his way home. I said I wondered what he would look like and if I would recognize him. She burst into tears and hugged me. I don't mind being hugged as long as it's not in front of any of my friends, but she was doing it so hard I could scarcely breathe. I didn't say anything, though.

When she had let go of me, I asked what time Daddy would be coming home. She said she didn't know, but she thought it might take quite a long time as Egypt is a long way away. Actually, it's 2,195 miles to Cairo. I worked it out on my *Bartholomew's Atlas* during a geography lesson last term. I don't know how far it is to Sidi Barrani where he is, though.

According to Major Stanford-Dingley, all the ships go from Alexandria which is at least 120 miles nearer, or anyway they did when he came home after fighting in the desert with Lawrence of Arabia. But even if the ship went at 12 knots all the way, it would still take a week and anyway, according to the Major, he won't be able to get off straight away.

I didn't say anything about it to Mummy as she is upset enough already.

Monday, May 7th

IN Chapel this morning The Chimp said, 'This is a great day in the history of Badger's Mount School. At 2.41 a.m. this morning in Rheims, the German Army Chief of Staff, General Alfred Jodl, signed the instrument of unconditional surrender at the headquarters of the Supreme Allied Commander, General Eisenhower. The General says that the German people and the German armed forces have been delivered into the victors' hands – and about time, too.'

We all cheered like mad and then The Chimp said a prayer to Jesus, the Supreme Allied Commander of the World, and said would the person who had drawn a picture of Chad looking like a monkey on the senior changing room wall with the words, 'Wot? No monkey nuts?' report to his study in Break.

When I got home tonight, Mummy and I listened to the news which said that Mr Churchill would not be broadcasting tonight. I was getting ready for bed when Mummy called out, 'Tomorrow's going to be Victory in Europe Day and Winnie's going to broadcast in the afternoon.'

Much more important is the fact that it's my birthday tomorrow. I hope she hasn't forgotten.

M Y twelfth birthday. Mummy was sitting at the table in the morning room when I came down. I thought she was going to say 'Happy Birthday', but all she kept saying was 'It's over', and staring out of the window. I asked her if she was feeling all right and she suddenly noticed I was there and got up and came over and hugged me really hard and cried and said, 'I can't believe it.'

I couldn't believe she had forgotten my birthday, but I didn't say anything in case she hadn't. Instead, I asked her if I had to go to school and she said yes. Then I reminded her it was my birthday. I didn't mean to, but I didn't feel like going to school as it's Double Maths with Stuffy Bedding on Tuesdays. She said it had gone clean out of her head, what with all the excitement and everything. Anyway she *had* bought me a present. It was exactly what I had asked for, an EDBee model aeroplane engine, like the one Colin's got. It runs on ethylene glycol and you start it by flicking the propellor with your finger. I've tried it lots of times in Colin's father's shed and I really know how to do it now, but you've got to move your finger away quickly when it fires or the propellor hits it really hard and it hurts quite a lot.

It's a pity it's only the 1cc model and not the 2cc like Colin's, but I expect it'll go just as well. Not as far, that's all. It's also a pity I haven't got an aeroplane to attach it to, but I've saved up 4*s* 6*d* from my newspaper round and the balsa wood kits in Brock's are only 2*s* 3*d* so I might get one of those. A Spitfire would be best.

Mummy rang up the school to say I had a bit of a temperature. The Headmaster wasn't there but Mrs Harris was and said that the school was closed for today and tomorrow and the boarders had been sent home. I wish Mummy hadn't made up the excuse about my temperature. Now I won't be able to use it again for ages.

I wanted to try out my engine, but I haven't got any fuel. I went down to Colin's after breakfast to see if he had any, but there was no one in, so I came back to the camp, which is where I am writing this. I'm quite enjoying writing it, actually, which is funny because I usually hate writing English essays for Mr Reader. In fact I might go on writing it and show it to Daddy when he gets back. I'm sure he'll be interested to know what Mummy and I've been doing while he's been away.

Julian wrote a diary once. He called it his Journal. He decided to start it after reading Robinson Crusoe who also wrote a journal. The trouble was he wanted me to be his Man Friday and I got fed up with being bossed around and he lost interest and threw it away. I bet he'll be jolly envious when he sees that I've started one. I might call mine a journal too. I wish Julian was here so we could talk about Hitler committing suicide, but he's a boarder now and he won't be home till half-term and I can't be fagged to write to him. His father's a Chindit in the jungle in Burma and I bet he knows all the best ways to kill people. Daddy killed lots of Germans when he was a Desert Rat with Monty which is as good as being a Chindit in my opinion, but he's been on the General Staff for a year now and has probably forgotten how.

Actually, I think Hitler probably shot himself. I would have done if I'd been him. It's much better than swallowing poison which is agony, according to Matron, or stabbing yourself, like Brutus did in *Julius Caesar*. Well, actually he got Strato to hold his sword and then ran onto it. Mr Reader said in English that it was probably quicker and more painless than it sounded. Wetherby-Brown said that it wouldn't have been quick or pain-less if Brutus had closed his eyes at the last moment or tripped or something and missed his aim, like The Chimp did when he was giving Dishforth six last week. Mr Reader said that *his* aim would put the archers at Agincourt to shame, as Wetherby-Brown would very soon discover for himself if he made any more stupid comments like that.

It's funny to think of the war being over. I've often wondered what it would feel like and now that it's happened, I feel just like I did before. I wonder if the greengrocer's in Oxted will start selling bananas now. Julian tried one once when he went to stay with the Goodmans in Bromley, and according to him they don't taste anything like as bad as they look. A bit slimy compared with real fruit, but quite sweet.

Mummy went round this afternoon taking down the black-out curtains. She said she had never been more glad to see the back of anything in her life, but when I said could I have them so Julian and I could make a tent like the Bedouin in the desert, she said certainly not and folded them up and put them away in the bottom drawer of the chest on the landing. She said it was for a rainy day, which was quite funny actually as it's been raining all morning. I hope the war hasn't turned her what Worms, our gardener, calls doolally tap. I wouldn't want to have a mother who goes round wobbling her head all the time, like Appleyard's.

Briggs swears it was because he suddenly caught sight of Mrs Appleyard standing next to the sight-screen wobbling her head that he was bowled out by Peskett's father in last year's Fathers' Match. If Peskett's father is anything like Peskett, he can only bowl worm-scarers, and anyone can get someone out with a worm-scarer. Even Briggs.

Mr Churchill came on the wireless after lunch and said that hostilities will end officially at one minute after midnight tonight and that the German war is at an end. Mummy and I jumped up and grabbed each other and danced round the morning room table. Then Mr Churchill said, 'We may allow ourselves a brief period of rejoicing but Japan with all her treachery and greed remains unsubdued, so let us not forget the toils that lie ahead.' Mummy and I both looked at each other and pulled a face. But then he said, 'Advance Britannia! Long live the cause of freedom! God save the King!' and we both cheered again and danced in and out of all the rooms until we were both completely out of breath and collapsed onto the settee in the drawing room.

Actually, I'm rather sorry the war's over. I quite enjoyed it, personally. I don't think my cousins did, but that's not surprising considering Uncle Tony was killed at Arnhem, and anyway they live much nearer London and had to sleep in an Anderson shelter in the garden which can't have been very comfortable. We had a thing like a big iron table in our dining room. It was called a Morrison shelter. We didn't have any actual air raids but one or two bombs got dropped and lots of used shell cases, and anyway the siren was always going off, so we often got under it, just in case. There are still quite a few shell cases lying around in the garden, but I've stopped collecting them now. Colin's shell collection is actually bigger than mine, but he doesn't have an RAF officer's cap like the one Barbara Kippax's father gave me just before he got shot down. I wonder if he's been let out of his prison camp yet.

There was a programme on the wireless the other day by a man who was with some British soldiers in tanks when they broke into two of the biggest prisoner-of-war camps, or Stalags as the

Germans call them. Some of them had been captured at Arnhem (not Uncle Tony, though, worst luck) but some had been there ever since being captured at Dunkirk. That's five years ago!

This chap said that a lot of them had been made to march there all the way from Poland because the Germans were frightened that they might have been set free by the Russians and made to sleep in the snow and left to die if they couldn't walk any further. The ones that got there were terribly ill and were only kept alive by parcels of food sent by the Red Cross. Luckily, by the time the army arrived, the prisoners had taken over and locked the guards up. They ought to send Gilbert over to knock their teeth down their throats.

I wonder if Mummy is thinking of keeping the Morrison shelter for a rainy day? She's probably waiting till Daddy comes home. He'll know what's for the best. I hope he brings me something from a dead German, like a pistol. A Mauser would be best, preferably a 7.63mm. Also I hope we have real eggs for breakfast.

After Mr Churchill's speech, Mummy and I walked down to Oxted to see what was happening. There was bunting strung across the roads and flags were hanging from lots of the windows. People were walking up and down waving little Union Jacks and singing things like 'There'll Always Be An England' and shouting and kissing each other. A whole lot of them had formed a line across the road outside Blades and were dancing down Station Road East and sweeping people up along the way.

We went round to Station Road West and got down to the Hoskins' Arms just as the Home Guard were marching past. The church bells were ringing and there were hundreds of children on the cricket pitch playing rounders and things. Lots of tables had been put up near the pavilion and ladies wearing red, white and blue flowers made of paper were putting out plates of sandwiches and jam tarts and jellies and blancmanges.

When they'd finished, someone rang a big bell and all the children stopped playing and rushed across to the tables and sat down and started tucking in. I asked Mummy if I could as well, but she said it was only meant for local children. I said that I'm a local child. We live in Fernhurst Road. She said that living locally is not the same thing as being a local child. I asked her what the difference is and she said that local children go to the local school and their parents don't live in the same sort of road as us. I said why not, and she said because they are working class and wouldn't want to live next door to people who talk with different accents from them and whose fathers wear bowler hats and travel up to the City on the 8.03, and whose mothers run the Women's Institute and whose children go to schools like Badger's Mount. Anyway, they probably couldn't afford to buy a house in Fernhurst Road. I said, what if they could? She said it wasn't just to do with money and nobody had any money at the moment anyway. People from different backgrounds don't mix and that's all there is to it. I said perhaps it might be fun if they did. She said, 'You've been spending too much time talking to Worms. The sooner your father comes home, the better.'

When we got home, we rang Colin to see if he wanted to come round for tea but there was no reply. Mummy got out a sponge cake she'd made with some powdered eggs she'd been saving and stuck some candles on it and sang 'Happy Birthday' and afterwards we played cricket. I scored 25 not out, most of them wides, and I got her out fourth ball, even though I was bowling left-handed and underarm.

Later I went down to the Penwardens' to see if Colin was back, but he wasn't. I was just leaving when he and his mother came in through the gate. I asked him where he'd been. He said, 'The children's party in Oxted. It was top line. There was tons to eat. I had three jellies and afterwards we were each given a shilling, an orange, a bag of crisps and some sweets. You should have come.'

Wednesday, May 9th

Accordng to Mrs Phipps, our daily, there's going to be a bonfire up on the Common on Saturday evening with fireworks and things. He said, 'Mind you, they did the same thing after the Kaiser's war and look where that got them.'

Anyway, I hope I'll be able to go. I went down to Colin's after tea to tell him and see if he was going. He said he didn't know. He never seems to know anything much. Nor do his parents. Last year Mrs Penwarden got packed up to go on holiday, stripped all the beds, finished off all the food in the larder and when she came down with the suitcases Mr Penwarden said, 'It's not till next week,' and got in the car and went off to play golf. When I asked Mummy why Colin's father wasn't in the war, she said he probably had a reserve occupation, which means he was doing vital work for the war effort, like being a spy or something. I can't imagine he'd have been a very good spy with a cough like his. Mummy says he smokes for England. Perhaps that's why he got a reserve occupation.

Thursday, May 10th

BACK to school, worst luck, *and* I've been put on report by Mr Wolf. It isn't fair. All I said was the Black Death started under the armpits and spread all over Europe and he said, 'Very funny, Hodge. Well, how about this for a joke? You're on report.' I also got a dead arm from Whittington, the captain of Kitchener's, for yawning in prayers. That was because Mummy let me stay up late last night to hear Tom Arnold's 'Hoop-La!' on the Forces Programme. Robb Wilton and Max Wall were on, with Jack Train, Harold Berens, Ted Ray and Harry Lester and his Hayseeds. I don't really like Robb Wilton. I think Colin's brother Rupert is much funnier.

Last Sunday Colin and I were in the little garage at his house trying to get his steam engine to go and when we tried to get out we found that Rupert had tied a huge rope right round the outside and we couldn't get the door open. Actually it wasn't as funny as all that as we had to wait till Colin's father came back from golf to let us out, but at least it was funnier than Robb Wilton. All he does is say 'The day war broke out' in a silly voice and everybody laughs, including Mummy. When I asked her what the joke was, she said, 'Once you try to explain a joke it isn't funny any more.' If you ask me, no one else gets it either and they only laugh because everyone else does.

'Children's Hour' was another boring Visit to Cowleaze Farm with Ralph Whitlock, so instead Colin put on the tin helmet he found in Staffhurst Wood and we went up to my house on our bikes and I put on my RAF cap and we played Dive-bombers. It's really good fun. We both get handfuls of berries and Colin stands behind the hedge outside his house and when I come tearing past on my bike he has to try and hit me with his berries and I have to try and hit him. As usual Mrs Freeman in Bombers shouted at us from behind her hedge and said that if we went on making so much noise she'd speak to our parents, so we had to stop.

Friday, May 11th

I T was meant to be *Henry IV* on the Home Service last night with Laurence Olivier and Ralph Richardson, but instead, Mr Churchill came on and gave a talk about the end of the war so I was allowed to stay up, though not for 'Victory Serenade' that came on afterwards.

I've never actually seen him, even though he lives quite near at Chartwell, but Colin did once. He was on a bike ride to Ide Hill when this black car came past hooting and somebody threw a cigar stub out of the window. Colin swears he saw a hand giving a V-for-Victory sign out of the back window.

Anyway, he picked up the stub and took it home and put it in a tin in the shed at the bottom of the garden. We got it out again the other day and thought about smoking it, but I didn't like the idea that it had been in someone else's mouth, even if it was Mr Churchill's, so we put it back again. Colin says it might be very valuable one day and that he might be able to sell it for enough money to buy a Raleigh Blue with drop handlebars. I wouldn't mind having a new bike, too. I quite like my green Hercules but it's really old now and bits of leather keep coming off the seat. Also, it doesn't have gears.

They had a play on 'Children's Hour' called 'Beau Brocade'. It was the story of a Derbyshire Highwayman. It wasn't as boring as Cowleaze Farm, but nearly.

Saturday, May 12th

T HIS afternoon we decorated the camp with some paper Union Jacks which Colin found in his attic and a picture of Mr Churchill which I cut out of the VE edition of the *Daily Express*. The good thing about having a camp in the middle of a lot of rhododendron bushes is that you can use the branches to stick things up with drawing pins. Also, because the leaves never fall off, you can't ever see through the branches so no one knows you're there.

I've suddenly thought: I hope Mummy wasn't keeping the *Daily Express* for anything. When you think about it, it could be quite valuable one day, though obviously not anything like as valuable as Mr Churchill's cigar.

I'M writing this under the bedclothes with a torch. I don't mean I'm writing it with a torch, I mean I'm holding a torch while I write it with a pencil. We've just come back from the bonfire on the Common. Colin came with us. It was quite good fun, actually. Someone had made a Guy Fawkes out of Hitler and when the head fell off everyone cheered. Funnily enough, I read in the paper that someone tried to burn Hitler's body after he committed suicide. There's a special word for this, but I can't remember what. Something to do with iron. Colin didn't know. I'll ask Mr Reader in English tomorrow.

There wasn't much to eat or drink, but there never is these days. In fact there seems to be less than there was during the war. Luckily, the Wyndhams over at Merle Common have chickens and they let us have some eggs from time to time. Mummy puts them in something called water-glass. According to Colin, it's sodium silicate. You mix it up with water and put the eggs in and it's supposed to keep them fresh.

You can also use it for making a crystal garden. I made a really good one once using copper sulphate crystals, bits of copper wire, etc. I was thinking of doing another one specially for when Daddy comes home, but they'd run out of crystals at the chemist's and didn't know when they'd be getting any more in. Mummy also doesn't know when the Wyndhams are going to sell us more eggs, so now we have to use powdered which taste a bit like sawdust. I've never actually eaten sawdust, but I imagine that's what it tastes like.

The best thing about the bonfire was the fireworks, but actually they weren't that good. There was only one rocket, which went up a bit and then suddenly shot off across the golf course and into a tree. Brigadier Williams who lives down the road said, 'I can piss further than that.' When I asked Mummy on the way home if she'd enjoyed herself she said she thought it was all a bit of a flop.

This afternoon there was a Service of Thanksgiving from St Paul's. The King and Queen were there. It's a pity Chimp Harris wasn't. His talk about Hitler and the rugger tackle would have cheered the whole thing up a lot, and his face would have got a good laugh too. Wetherby-Brown swears he once looked through the Harrises' sitting room window and saw The Chimp and his wife grooming each other. In fact, he's thinking of ringing the people at the Zoo and telling them that two of their exhibits have escaped from the Monkey House and would they send a couple of keepers down to collect them.

Monday, May 14th

IF Mummy thinks life is dull she ought to come to school and try one of Mr Reader's English lessons. This morning he gave us a piece from Macaulay's essay on Warren Hastings and we had to read it and answer questions on it. One of the questions was 'Pick out a noun clause in apposition to the subject.' When I asked what was the point of knowing things like this, Mr Reader said, 'The point, Hodge, is that it is part of the Common Entrance syllabus.'

After the lesson I asked him what the word is you use to describe Hitler being burnt in real life and then being burnt on a bonfire. 'Bloody good show,' he said.

Wednesday, May 16th

SOME of the tadpoles have started to grow tails. They're just tiny stumps at the moment, but they definitely weren't there yesterday when I looked.

Thursday, May 17th

THEY'VE all grown tails now and quite a few have wriggled out of the jelly and into the water.

Friday, May 18th

THEY'RE all out now. They don't do much except shoot about all over the place. Sometimes they just float with their tails pointing downwards, not moving, as if they were standing at attention, then they start to sink very slowly and just before they get to the bottom they suddenly shoot off again. It's quite nice having them as pets, though actually I would prefer a dog, or even a guinea pig.

Saturday, May 19th

COLIN and I were playing Dive-bombers this morning at the top of the road when a removals van drove into Meadowcroft. We were watching the men unloading the van when a Jowett Javelin drove up and two girls got out with their mother and started getting suitcases out of the boot. One's about the same age as us, but the mother looks even older than Mummy.

She called out, 'I like your Air Force cap,' but I couldn't be fagged to say anything back, so we went off on our bikes. Colin did lots of really high bumps with his front wheel and I went quite a long way without holding onto the handlebars, but when we stopped and looked back they'd disappeared. Typical girls.

Sunday, May 20th

COLIN and I went down to the stream and got some more weed for the tadpoles. They really seem to like it, though they mostly eat mud. Colin says that's because it's full of nourishment. I can't imagine why. It reminded me of the time Julian's cousin Morag came to stay and we were having a picnic tea in the tent in the garden and when nobody was looking we took the tomato out of the sandwiches and put worms in instead and told her it was potted meat and she ate it.

Wednesday, May 23rd

I CAME home after school to find Mummy looking really upset and having a gin, even though it was only five o'clock. She tried to pretend it was water but I could smell it wasn't. When I asked her if something had happened to Daddy she said, 'It's

nothing to do with Daddy. It's Mr Churchill. He's resigned.
There's going to be a General Election on July 5th and if Mr
Attlee wins, he'll be Prime Minister instead.' I said I thought
Mr Churchill was always going to be Prime Minister. 'So did
I, darling,' said Mummy. 'We all did.' I hope this doesn't mean
Colin won't be able to sell his cigar stub now.

Friday, May 25th

GRANNY Hodge has come for a few days. She's been staying
in London with Auntie Susan. She often stays there.
Mummy says it makes her feel a bit less sad about Uncle Tony
and she likes taking Maureen and Milo to Fuller's and having
walnut cake. Daddy's got another brother called Wilfred who
lives in Brighton. I've never met him and no one ever talks
about him. He's never got married and when I asked Mummy
why, she said it's because he's a confirmed bachelor and I'm
not to mention his name to Granny because it upsets her.

Anyway, I really like it when she comes. She lets me go
through her handbag which is always full of face powder and
smells just like Granny. The best thing is her lucky rabbit's foot.
It has still got its claws on but is very soft and also smells of face
powder. I also like it when she comes because she takes me to
the pictures. She goes a lot in the afternoons where she lives in
London and if there are any children waiting around outside
and it's an A-film, she lets them go in with her. She's never
taken me to see an A-film. When I asked her why once, she
said, 'Whatever would your mother think of me?'

I'd really like to see an A-film one day. Julian saw one last
holidays in London with his aunt and said it was quite boring
and had quite a lot of kissing in it. I said I didn't think kissing
boring and he said, 'Well it is, so there.' When I asked Granny
if it was, she said it depends who's doing the kissing. For
example, Franchot Tone is a better kisser than Ronald
Colman. I said how about Clark Gable, and she said, 'So-so.'

The film I'd like to see most is *Objective Burma* with Errol
Flynn. These two teams of soldiers get dropped behind Jap
lines to destroy a radar station, but when they get to the airstrip
to be picked up something goes wrong and they have to make
their own way back through 150 miles of jungle. One lot get
caught and tortured but the others with Errol Flynn get

through. I bet there isn't much kissing in that.

Anyway, I bet I'll finish up being taken to see something like *National Velvet* with Mickey Rooney and this girl Elizabeth Taylor, or, even worse, *The Lights of Old Santa Fe* with Roy Rogers and Trigger. I hate horses, I hate films about them, and I hate Trigger. I'm not very keen on Roy Rogers, either.

Granny says a lot of people she knows only go to the pictures to see the main attraction but she never misses the supporting programme which is often better than the main picture. She thinks the *Topical Budget* is the best bit of all. She says it saves her having to read the newspapers.

One of the best things we do when she's here is go through my collection of film star cigarette cards. She knows even more about film stars than Matron does, what films they've been in, who they've been married to etc. I bet not many people know that Merle Oberon was born in Tasmania and that her real name is Estelle Thompson, or that Ida Lupino's father was a famous clown, or that Anna Neagle was once a gym teacher, though now I think about it, she does look a bit like Miss Longcroft at our school.

Actually, I'm thinking of writing to 'Children's Hour' and saying that I am the school expert on film stars and asking if I can be on Regional Round. The only trouble is, Uncle Mac sounds just like Mr Reader, and when I told him at lunch the other day that Dolores Del Rio is second cousin to Ramon Navarro, he said, 'Shut up and get on with your fish.'

It's a pity Granny doesn't know a bit more about Aircraft of the Royal Air Force or Railway Equipment. She said she had never heard of the slip-coach system or 120-ton crocodile waggon, and that she hadn't the foggiest idea how to shunt a train by capstan or how a vacuum brake works. 'Just as long as it does, that's all that matters,' she said. I think she might get on quite well with Mr Reader.

This evening we listened to 'Music Hall' on the wireless. Arthur Askey was on. According to Atwater, whose aunt knows Anne Ziegler and Webster Booth, he's smaller than Gore-Andrews' brother who's only eleven. He sounds like it. Peter Brough and Archie Andrews were on, too. I've often wondered if Peter Brough moves his mouth when he's on the wireless. When I asked Granny, she said, 'I once saw him at the Tooting Empire and he moved his lips all the time.'

If you ask me, it's pretty stupid having a ventriloquist on the wireless in the first place. In fact, it's about as stupid as putting on a Charlie Chaplin film in the middle of 'Variety Bandbox'. They never have actually, but if they did, I mean. When I said that to Mummy she said, 'Let's face it, it's pretty stupid having a show on the wireless starring a lump of wood.'

Saturday, May 26th

COLIN came round and we played cricket in the garden. He was Compton and I was Miller, using the long run-up through the rose garden and the gap in the macrocarpa hedge. He scored 20, mostly cow-shots, and then I changed to being Doug Wright and caught him playing back to a leg break that was much too well pitched up.

When we changed round, I was Compton and he was Miller. I played some quite good leg glances into the raspberries and then hit a really hard off-drive into the herbaceous border and broke some delphiniums and Mummy told us to stop, so we went for a bike ride on the Common instead and then went back to Colin's and read his *Radio Fun* Annuals.

Sunday, May 27th

I GOT a puncture on the Common and arrived at school late for Evensong and had to sit at the back with Matron and Mrs Harris. Holmes-Johnson was pumping the organ, as usual, when the handle came off in the middle of the 'The Day Thou Gavest Lord Is Ended' and we had to sing the rest of it while The Chimp went 'La la la' in a loud voice. I couldn't sing properly because Mrs Harris smelt so strongly of scent I had to keep holding my breath. Afterwards I overheard Wetherby-Brown's mother saying to Wetherby-Brown's father, 'Did you see Mrs Harris? She was wearing more make-up than Coco the Clown at Bertram Mills' Circus.' Wetherby-Brown's father said, 'So *that's* where all our school fees go!'

When I told Wetherby-Brown, he said, 'What the parents don't realise is that the real reason she wears so much make-up is to disguise the fact that she's a chimp.'

JUNE

Saturday, June 2nd

THIS afternoon Colin and I were on our bikes on Limpsfield Chart when we were chased by a gang of boys on bikes who wanted to bash us up. Luckily we escaped down Robinswood Lane and through the Johnsons' garden. Colin said they were village boys and that he'd seen them before, but I think they were Japs. I'm sorry Julian's father wasn't here. He'd have known how to deal with them. I cycled down to ask Mrs Harrington whether she had heard when he was coming home and she said she couldn't see the Japanese giving up easily and he could be out there in Burma for years. She asked if we had had any news about Daddy and when I said no she said she wondered if she would recognise Colonel Harrington after such a long time. I think she must have been joking, though actually she looked quite sad.

Tuesday, June 5th

LAST night Granny and I listened to 'Monday Night at Eight' with Anona Winn. I mean, Anona Winn did the programme. I quite like Richard Murdoch and Puzzle Corner, but the bit called 'With a Star and a Song' with Peter Cavanagh was boring. He did imitations of people like Issy Bonn and the Finkelfeffer Family, and Vic Oliver, which sounded quite like them, but not as much as they would have done if the people themselves had been on. I don't know why they weren't, really. Granny said her next-door neighbour had once met Issy Bonn. When I asked what he was like, Granny said, 'I didn't ask and she didn't tell me.'

I'd quite like to be on the wireless myself when I grow up. It must be really interesting meeting people like Nosmo King and Norman and Henry Bones, the boy detectives, and Vic Oliver. According to Granny, Nosmo King isn't really called that at all, he's called something completely different and only called himself Nosmo King because he saw a No Smoking sign. It's obvious when you think about it. When I told Colin, he said he couldn't understand what I was talking about. I sometimes wonder why I'm friends with Colin at all. I also wonder what it must be like for Mr Churchill to have Vic Oliver as his son-in-law. When I asked Granny, she said, 'Not easy.'

Wednesday, June 6th

I REALLY hate Tub. The water's always freezing cold and a funny browny-greeny colour and smells of something funny. Yesterday I was standing in the shallow end when a frog swam past. One of the worst bits is changing. The changing rooms smell just like Wetherby-Brown's feet. I wish I had a shiny green bathing costume like Pilbrow's instead of mine which is made of maroon wool and has a white belt with a shiny buckle sort of thing with sharp teeth and you have to push the end of the belt through and I never can. Also, the wool is frightfully bristly and whenever I put it on it always feels damp, even though it's been hanging up for days, and when I get out, it's so full of water it hangs down almost as far as my knees and everyone laughs and makes quacking noises, which is stupid because if I really was a duck I'd be able to swim without having to be held up by a strap on the end of a stick and be shouted at by Mr Bentham.

The other night I dreamt I could do swallow dives like Johnny Weissmuller did off that high rock in the Tarzan film we saw last term, but although I stood for ages on the diving board, I couldn't move at all. Mr Bentham saw me and shouted, 'It's only water, laddie. It won't bite you.' In the end I got off and went down to the shallow end and climbed down the steps as usual. I tried dog-paddling and managed to go for about a yard but then I swallowed a whole lot of water and had to stop. I thought at first I might have swallowed the frog and was very nearly sick. I was standing there coughing and spit-ting and trying to rub the water out of my eyes when Mr Bentham walked across and said, 'You know your trouble, laddie?' I said, 'Don't kick my legs enough, sir?' 'No,' he said. 'You're wet. That's your trouble. You're too bloody wet.' Dishforth who was standing nearby said, 'We're all wet, sir.' Mr Bentham said, 'There's wet and there's wet,' and pushed him in.

I bet Johnny Weissmuller didn't have to put up with this sort of thing when he learnt to swim. But then, being an American, he probably didn't have to wear a maroon woollen bathing costume.

Friday, June 8th

IN Break today I told Mr Reader what Granny had said about Nosmo King and he said, 'A man once came up to the Duke of Wellington and said, "Mr Smith, I presume?" Do you know what the Duke of Wellington said?' I said no. Mr Reader said, '"If you believe that, you'll believe anything."' I was going to tell him about my journal, but I couldn't be fished.

Saturday, June 9th

DADDY's birthday. He's thirty-six. I wish I could have sent him a card, but I don't suppose they have postmen in Sidi Barrani. This morning we put Granny on the train and went shopping. We never went to the pictures in the end, so instead she gave me a book token. She cried when she said goodbye.

Afterwards we went to the Co-op. I like going there because when you pay, they put the money into a special little can which they attach to a wire on the ceiling and then they pull a wooden handle on the end of a chain and the can goes flying across the ceiling on the wire to the lady in the cashier's desk. She takes the tin down, puts the change in and sends the tin whizzing back. Mummy says it's an example of modern science and reckons that one day all shops will have it.

We were in Brock's later, buying a Worzel Gummidge with the book token, when we bumped into Mrs Masterson-Smith with Anthony, looking really goofy in his new giglamps. I asked him what he was doing home in the middle of term and he said, 'Things.' Mummy said, 'Hallo, Jean. Any news of John?' Mrs Masterson-Smith said she was expecting him home any day but that he was going to have to go back to Germany after a week or so. Anthony said, 'We're not allowed to say why. It's hush-hush.' Typical Anthony trying to make his father sound more important than he really is. I bet *he* never met Monty – or anyone else important, come to that.

I thought we were going to go straight home but Mrs Masterson-Smith invited Mummy to have morning coffee with her in Bobby's. I hate the smell of coffee. Mummy says it isn't real coffee, it's only coffee essence and that when things get going, it'll be possible to buy real coffee again and I'll really like the smell then. It doesn't make the coffee at Bobby's smell any better. I said I'd walk home but Mummy said that Anthony was staying and that it would be rude if I didn't too, so I had to sit there with them for ages, listening to Mummy and Mrs Masterson-Smith talking about clothes coupons and staring at Anthony's ugly phizog. I know he's meant to be brainy, but he's not as brainy as all that in my opinion. At Martin Howard's birthday party when I asked him to name all the ranks of all the officers in the RAF, the silly fool put Group Captain above Air Commodore. Then he bet me I couldn't name the titles of all the books written by Charles Dickens. I bet him threepence I could. Actually I could only think of six, but luckily I remembered the names of some of the books I'd seen on the shelf in Mr Reader's room when he was reading to us last term, like *Mansfield Park* and *The Golden Bowl* and *Jude the Obscure*, and added them. Anthony said, 'Okay, you win,' and handed me a threepenny bit.

Mrs Masterson-Smith said, 'Oh, by the way, I've been meaning to tell you, I've found this marvellous little woman who runs things up for me.' Anthony said, 'Last week she made Mummy a skirt out of one of the drawing room curtains.' I said, 'How do you draw the curtains now?' Anthony said, 'Tightly,' and sniggered.

They were just paying the bill when the lady who has moved in at Meadowcroft just up the road walked in through the door with her two daughters. Mrs Masterson-Smith said, 'Well, if it isn't Marjorie Pardoe!' As they were crossing the room towards us, Anthony went bright red. His mother said, 'Take your glasses off, Ant.' He said, 'Why should I?' She said, 'First impressions count.' Anthony said, 'You know

I can't see a thing without my glasses.' His mother said, 'As long as they can see *you*,' and she reached forward and took his glasses off and put them in her handbag. Mummy said to me, 'Don't stare, darling, it's rude.'

Mrs Masterson-Smith called out, 'Marjorie! What are you doing here? I thought you were living in a flat in Chelsea!' She said, 'I was, until Nigel went off with a Wren in the Admiralty.' Anthony's mother said in French, *'Attention les enfants.'* I was quite surprised. I didn't know grown-ups could speak French.

Mrs Pardoe said, 'Anyway, to cut a long story short, I decided to come and live down here. The girls and I have just moved into a house in Fernhurst Road.' Mummy said, '*We* live in Fernhurst Road. Which house are you?' Mrs Pardoe said, 'Meadowcroft. We've got a paddock at the back.' Mrs Masterson-Smith said, 'Do you have a horse?' Mrs Pardoe said, 'The girls have a pony. He's called Tommy.' I said, 'Is he named after Tommy Handley?' Mrs Masterson-Smith said, 'No.' Mummy said, 'We're in Monkswood.'

Mrs Pardoe introduced her daughters. The one who's about my age is called Jill and her sister's called Tessa. She said, 'Do you like ponies?' I said, 'It depends.' I heard Anthony sniggering but I didn't take any notice. She said, 'You must come round one day.' I said 'Thank you' without really meaning to. Tessa said, 'Don't forget to bring your RAF cap.' Anthony sniggered even louder.

Mrs Masterson-Smith said to the girls, 'Perhaps you might like to come to Hoofprints and play with Anthony one day?' Jill said, 'Do you have a pony?' Mrs Masterson-Smith said, 'No, but we've got a very nice croquet lawn.' Jill said, 'Ah.' Anthony went even redder than before and said, 'Actually I'm not very good at playing with people,' and he turned and walked into a chair which fell over with a crash and so did he. I tried not to laugh but I did anyway.

Thursday, June 14th

DISHFORTH has gone to hospital to have his tonsils and adenoids out, so I was picked for the 1st XI against Combe Park.

Major Stanford-Dingley went with us in the charabanc. It took over an hour to get there. On the way, Wetherby-Brown made a very good joke about Matron's bum looking like two barrage balloons stuck together and everybody laughed, including the driver. The Major said, 'I'll have you know that Combe Park is a very religious school and their headmaster does not take kindly to smut,' and gave him a detention.

When we arrived, their team was waiting for us in the drive. Their cricket master looked quite like Stan Laurel. As he was shaking the Major's hand he was sick all over his suede shoes and carried on talking as if nothing had happened.

We batted first and I scored seven and was hit really hard on the hand by their fastest bowler. Those rubber spikes on the gloves never work. It hurt so much I thought I must have broken my finger, but Major Stanford-Dingley who was umpiring at square leg looked at it and said, 'Nothing much wrong with that that a half-century on the board wouldn't put right.' The next ball was a head-high bumper, so I ducked. Unfortunately the ball nicked the top edge of my bat and I was caught at long-hop. As I was going out, the Major shouted, 'Fat lot of help you'd have been with Lawrence at Mudowwara!'

We were all out for 52 and their opening batsmen scored 53 for no wickets, mostly in boundaries.

Afterwards we had tea in the dining room which was very dark and full of statues of saints with haloes on the backs of their heads. A lot looked as if they were praying. One was of a man without many clothes on and lots of arrows sticking out of his body. He looked like Stuffy Bedding in one of his Maths bates.

For tea we had fish-paste sandwiches. They smelt a bit like the games master's sick. Pilbrow ate three. After that we had bright green blancmange which tasted of nothing at all, but smelt a bit like the sandwiches. After tea, their headmaster came in and gave a short talk about how God loves losers just as much as winners. He said, 'There is more joy in Heaven over one batsman that gets out first ball to a full toss than ninety-nine who score fifty, hold three catches and take four for twenty.' Major Stanford-Dingley said in quite a loud voice, 'Not at Badger's Mount, there isn't.' Everyone laughed. Their headmaster didn't, though.

The journey back in the coach wasn't very nice because of the smell of sick from the Major's shoes. No one dared to say anything so in the end we told Pilbrow to do it and said that if he didn't, the whole team would give him a Chinese burn. So

Pilbrow went to the front of the bus where the Major was sitting and said, 'Sir, it's a bit stuffy in here, could we open a window?' The Major said, 'Stuffy? You don't know what the word means. You should spend a night in a tent with half a dozen Bedouin who haven't washed for three months if you want to know what stuffy means.' Whittington said, 'Sir, is that where the expression stuffy bedding comes from?' Everybody laughed because of it being the nickname of our Maths master. The Major said, 'I'll give you stuffy bedding,' and he was just about to get up when Pilbrow was sick straight into his lap. It was bright green.

I hope Dishforth doesn't get well for ages and that I don't get put back into the 2nd XI.

Saturday, June 16th

THIS morning I came up the road with Ted in the milk cart. He let me take the reins for a bit. I felt a bit like Pompey the Great in his chariot riding into Rome in triumph after subduing Mithridates of Pontus, except that Pompey didn't have to keep stopping while someone hopped on and off with bottles of milk.

Sunday, June 17th

COLIN came round to help us get the car off the blocks. It's been in the garage for three years and the battery is completely flat, so we weren't able to get it going straightaway, but Colin's father lent us his battery charger and we put it on and left it charging until tomorrow morning. He says ours is the only Lanchester he has come across in the whole of Oxted and it is really in very good condition, considering. I still wish we had a Vauxhall Tourer like the Penwardens. I really enjoy sitting in the dicky seat with Colin.

We pushed the Lanchester out of the garage and then Mr Penwarden went in with Mummy to have some sherry and Colin and I sat in the front seat and pretended to drive it. Colin explained that Lanchesters and Daimlers have fluid fly-wheels and pre-selector gears. The lever is on the side of the steering wheel. All you do is put it against the number of the gear you want next, push the clutch in and out twice and it changes automatically. It's much easier to use than an ordinary gear, but you can't free-wheel down steep hills like you can in other cars. You can't do anything at the moment without the battery, but Colin says it will be charged by tomorrow lunchtime. He's coming round tomorrow evening after school to help us put it back in the car. I do hope it starts. It would be awful if Daddy came home and he didn't have a car to drive. I wonder if he's shaved off his moustache yet. In his last letter he said he would as soon as the war was over.

Saturday, June 23rd

COLIN came round after lunch and we listened in to the Second Victory Test Match between England and Australia from Bramall Lane, Sheffield. Hutton made 11, and Washbrook made 63. Hammond was 98 not out at tea. I'm really sorry Denis Compton's not playing. According to Colin he's still in the Army. He thinks he might be in India, but he's not sure.

After tea we got the car going. I thought at first it wasn't going to start and so did we all, but luckily Mr Henriksen from over the road happened to call in and turned the starting handle while Mummy and Colin fiddled with the ignition and mixture knobs. Tons of black smoke came out of the exhaust when it fired and Mummy thought for a moment it had caught on fire and screamed and jumped out, but then it started to run properly and we all went out for a ride.

It's been such a long time since Mummy's driven that she couldn't think where to go, so we just drove round for a bit until we came to the Royal Oak at Merle Common, near where Mr Tooth's farm track meets the main road. Mummy said why didn't we stop for a celebration drink, so we did. We sat on a wooden bench outside looking across Mr Tooth's fields to the spire of Crowhurst church in the distance. Mummy and Mr Henriksen had some beer and Colin and I had orange squash. It was quite weak, though not as weak as Mummy makes it at home. I hope that now the war's over we'll have stronger orange squash.

Mr Henriksen said wasn't it a lovely peaceful evening and wasn't it nice to think that we wouldn't have to worry about pulling the black-out curtains any more and hearing about Hitler all the time and eating whale-meat casserole. Mummy said it was lovely, but not quite what she had expected. Mr Henriksen asked what she had expected and she said she didn't know, but she didn't think it was going to be like this.

What Mummy really meant was that it was much more boring than she had expected and I agree with her, but she couldn't say that to Mr Henriksen because the Danish people were invaded by the Germans and some of Mr Henriksen's relations were sent away and never seen again, including his mother and his sister.

His mother must have been really old because Mr Henriksen is bald on top with grey hair and his wife died years ago. There is a picture of her on one of the tables in his house. It was obviously taken when she was young. She's wearing an evening dress with a huge row of pearls, and a band round her forehead with a feather sticking up out of the front of it like a Red Indian. Her hair looks like corrugated iron.

Tuesday, June 26th

WE had herrings and cabbage for lunch which made me feel sick, followed by tapioca pudding which made me feel even sicker. I was about to ask if I could be excused when The Chimp came in and told us it had just been announced on the wireless that Lord Haw-Haw is going to be tried for treason. He said, 'If I had my way, he'd be dragged through London on a hurdle and hanged, drawn and quartered in the middle of Piccadilly Circus.' Wetherby-Brown asked him what being drawn and quartered meant and when The Chimp told us, Wetherby-Brown had to ask to be excused.

He then said that as a celebration of the defeat of Nazism,

yellow-livered cowardice and general lack of backbone, there would be no afternoon school and instead there would be an inter-house British Bulldog Competition on Lower Field. It was really good fun. Trenchard's beat Kitchener's in the final and Haig's and Jellicoe's came third and fourth and the losers had to run round the field ten times, except for Wetherby-Brown who had to do it fifteen times for asking to be excused and showing moral slackness.

Friday, June 29th

THE tadpoles are getting quite large. I've moved them into a much bigger jar, but even so, most of them are over an inch long and some are beginning to grow tiny legs. Mummy says it's cruel to go on keeping them in captivity and that I ought to put them back in the stream where they belong. I might keep them just a bit longer. At least they're safe on the window ledge.

JULY

Sunday, July 1st

A TERRIBLE thing happened this morning. I was sitting at the morning room table translating a bit from Caesar's Gallic Wars and wondering why *nostri* always seem to win, when there was a loud crash from the kitchen. I rushed in to find that the Ballards' cat had jumped in through the open window and knocked the tadpole jar onto the draining board. The sink was full of wriggling black shapes. I managed to rescue most of them but a lot slid down the plug-hole before I could get hold of them. Mummy says they'll probably survive all right, but I can't stop thinking about them being swept down miles and miles of pipe in the dark, not knowing where they are or where they're going. I've put the survivors back in the stream and they looked really pleased. I really wish I'd done it yesterday. If I do get another pet, I'm definitely not going to get a cat.

When I told Colin what had happened, he said creatures that live in water always survive and he'd read a story in a magazine once about a man in New York who had some baby alligators that escaped down the lavatory and now the sewers are full of huge crocodiles that come up through the manholes in the night and eat people.

With a bit of luck Oxted might soon be overrun by killer frogs.

34

Monday, July 2nd

I N Double Latin today Gnasher Davies spent the whole of the first lesson teaching us how to decline the pluperfect subjunctive active of *duco* – 'would that I had led'. It goes *duxissem, duxisses, duxisset, duxissemus, duxissetis, duxissent.*

When he asked if anyone could give an example of the pluperfect subjunctive in English, Pilbrow put his hand up and said, 'Wood that I had chopped, sir?' Gnasher said, 'Pilbrow, the Romans mastered half the world without cracking a single joke. Surely you can do the same with the pluperfect subjunctive?'

Wetherby-Brown said, 'I know a Roman joke, sir.' Gnasher said, 'In that case, Brown, don't hesitate to share it with us.' Wetherby-Brown said, '*Caesar adsum jam forte. Pompey aderat.*' Everyone laughed. Gnasher said, 'I don't wish to be a wet-blanket, Brown, but the fact of the matter is that your joke, excellent though it is in its way, only works in English.' Wetherby-Brown said, 'But, sir, that was real Latin.' Gnasher said, 'Have you ever considered a career in music hall?' Wetherby-Brown said, 'No, sir.' Gnasher said, 'I'm very glad to hear it.'

The trouble with masters is that they always think they're much funnier than they really are.

Thursday, July 5th

E LECTION Day. In Chapel this morning, The Chimp said a special prayer for Mr Churchill and the Conservatives. He put in lots of 'thees' and 'thous' but even so you could tell that he had made it up himself. He said, 'Thou knowest, Lord, as well as we do that there is only one man for the job. Lettest not Thou the Labour lot get in and muck everything up. For God's sake. Amen.'

Friday, July 6th

I N Break we all had to go to the dining room and sit in front of a blackboard with the words CONSERVATIVE, LABOUR and LIBERAL written up on it in different-coloured chalk – blue for Conservative, red for Labour and yellow for Liberal. Labour were miles ahead but The Chimp said that didn't mean anything and we would have to wait until all the results came in from the soldiers and sailors and airmen who are still overseas, and that just because a lot of people in England had taken leave of their senses, it didn't follow that everyone else had too. Seabrook put his hand up and said that his parents had voted for Mr Attlee and they weren't mad. The Chimp said, 'We'll see about that', and told him to go and stand outside his study. After a while he went out too and there was a long silence and then Seabrook came back in looking red in the face. He held up four fingers and went and stood by the window. Everyone looked at him but he didn't blub or anything. After a while The Chimp came back in again and said, 'Think yourself lucky, Seabrook. Lord Haw-Haw won't get off so lightly.'

Tuesday, July 10th

I N Maths today Stuffy Bedding was telling us how to express decimal points as fractions when Holmes-Johnson let off really loudly. Stuffy said, 'What exactly was that meant to be?' Holmes-Johnson said, 'A vulgar fraction, sir.' Stuffy completely blew up and threw him out of the window into a rose bed and he had to go to Matron and have a whole lot of thorns taken out of his bum. It's jolly lucky the Form III classroom's on the ground floor, otherwise he might have been hurt.

Saturday, July 14th

M RS Pardoe telephoned while we were having breakfast to ask Mummy if she'd like to pop up to Meadowcroft and have coffee and look round and would I like to go too and play with the girls in the garden. I said that actually I wanted to listen in to the Third Victory Test from Lord's. She said it would be on later and I wouldn't be missing much anyway with Denis Compton not playing.

I said I'd suddenly remembered Colin and I were going to go down to Oxted on our bikes to buy the balsa-wood aeroplane kits we've been saving up for. She said we could do that after lunch. I said what if we got there and found that Brock's had sold them this morning? She said why didn't I ring up and ask them to hold them for us? I said that actually my bike had got a slow puncture in the back tyre.

She said that if I got up straight away and had my breakfast I could have it mended and ready in time to use after lunch. I said that actually I'd suddenly remembered I'd run out of rubber solution. She said in that case I wouldn't be able to go anyway and as I hadn't got anything better to do I could go with her to the Pardoes', they seemed a very nice family and it was high time I made some new friends. I said that I already had enough friends. She said you can never have enough friends.

I said that I'd suddenly remembered Colin had a spare tube of rubber solution and why didn't I nip down and ask if I can borrow it? She said I could do that *after* we'd been to the Pardoes'. I said that I didn't think the girls would want to play cricket or Dive-bombers or anything like that and she said, 'You have a simple choice: either you come with me to the Pardoes' or you stay shut in your room.' I said in that case I'd come with her.

When we got there at about eleven Mrs Pardoe said, 'Oh, the girls didn't think for a moment you'd come, so Jill's gone for a ride on Tommy and Tessa's spending the day with a friend.' I said that I'd only come to say that I couldn't come and that actually I had arranged to spend the day with a friend, too. I didn't look at Mummy when I said this because I knew she would give me one of her looks. Mrs Pardoe didn't seem to mind and said, 'Well, come in and have an orange squash and a quick look round first.'

Their house isn't nearly as nice as ours. There aren't any pictures on the walls and the curtains in the drawing room look like the opposite of Mrs Masterson-Smith's – i.e., as if they had been made from someone's old skirts.

Mrs Pardoe said, 'The house is jolly cold and jolly rackety, but it's got lovely oak floors and tiles in the hall and I thought to myself, a few of mama's Persian rugs scattered around and we could move in tomorrow, which we did.'

Afterwards she took us round the garden, which is quite nice, though not as nice as ours. The lawn is just big enough for a cricket pitch, but there's nowhere for a fast bowler to do a Gubby Allen-type run-up, unless you run along the side of the hedge and then turn right just before you get to the wicket and Gubby could never have taken 10 for 40 against Lancashire if he'd done that. It's a pity he isn't playing for us at Lord's today. We don't have any fast bowlers unless you count Edrich, which I don't, really.

At the bottom of the garden they've got a swimming-pool. It isn't very big and there isn't any water in it. The concrete round the outside is cracked and there's grass growing through, just like Tub, but Mrs Pardoe says she's going to fill it up soon and why don't I come round one day and have a dip? Luckily Mummy was looking at the rose garden at the time or she might have said that I didn't know how to swim, so I just said thanks, I'd think about it.

After lunch I got my bike out to go down to Colin's. I was just pedalling off down the drive when Mummy came out of the kitchen door, so I had to hop off and quickly let the back tyre down. I don't think she noticed. It was a frightful fag having to push it all the way down the road and when I got there I found Colin had gone out to see his aunt at Crockham Hill, so I pumped the tyre up again and rode down to Brock's. There weren't any Spitfires left, they'd sold the last one in the morning, so I bought a Hurricane instead which is almost as good as a Spitfire, but not quite.

I've been thinking about the Pardoes' pool. I might go round for a swim or I might not. It depends. I'm definitely not going to go when there's a Test Match on. Hutton made 104 this morning and I missed the whole thing.

Sunday, July 15th

THIS evening they are going to turn on all the lights in London again. I asked Mummy if we could go and see them, but she said she hadn't got enough coupons to go galli-vanting round the countryside and that we'd have to wait till Daddy comes home and all go up together.

Colin came round in the afternoon. I showed him my Hurricane kit and he said he'd got a Spitfire. He bought it in Brock's yesterday morning, it was the last one they had. Why didn't we go down to his house and start putting them together?

While we were glueing the wings, I told him about the Pardoes' swimming-pool. He said that his aunt and uncle in Edenbridge had a pool and that he once saw his cousin Amanda swimming in it completely bare. She's only twelve and a half, but Colin says she's very well developed for her age and not too fat. I think I might definitely go round to the Pardoes' for a swim after all, but I'm not going to tell Colin.

Monday, July 16th

THE house was empty when I got back from school. I looked all round, but although lots of the windows were wide open there was definitely no one there. Then I heard someone singing in the garden. It was Mummy picking raspberries. I called out and she came rushing up the lawn with her arms wide open and grabbed me and swung me round until we were both dizzy and fell over in a heap.

When she had got her breath back, she said, 'Guess what? Daddy's coming home next week. I got a telegram from him this morning.' And she burst into tears and hugged me so hard I got my face stuck between her bosoms and couldn't breathe. She seems to cry a lot these days and I'm always being suffocated.

When she finally let go, I asked her if he would be here in time for the Fathers' Cricket Match which is next Thursday. She said she didn't know, he hadn't said exactly which day he was coming, but she'd ring up the War Office in the morning and try and find out. I really hope he does because he's supposed to be a brilliant batsman and opened for Oxford in 1933 and I'm sure they'd want him to play. If they do, I'll definitely be picked for the school team. They always pick you if your father's playing.

I have definitely decided to give Daddy the Hurricane as a welcome-home present. I hope he likes it. I also hope I finish it in time.

Australia won the Test by four wickets and Miller was 71 not out. The sooner Denis Compton gets back from India, the better.

Tuesday, July 17th

IT's very late and I should really be asleep, but I'm not sleepy at all. After supper Mummy and I went for a little walk. We were just coming up Fernhurst Road when we saw Worms coming in the opposite direction. As we got nearer we could see that his cheeks were wet with tears. Mummy was really worried and asked him what had happened. Had someone died? Worms said, 'Oh, Mrs Hodge, I was walking through the woods at the bottom of your garden on my way home from the Haycutter and I heard a nightingale singing, and it was the most beautiful sound I have ever heard.'

Wednesday, July 18th

MUMMY rang the War Office this morning and they said Daddy's ship is expected to arrive in Liverpool some time on Sunday and he will travel down as soon as possible. She says that means he should be home on Monday afternoon. He'll probably catch a train from Victoria. I said I hoped I'd be home in time to go to the station and shall we pick him up in the Lanchester? She said she didn't know what train he would be on, but she expected he would ring us when he got to London, and if he did arrive before I got home, I'd be able to come in and surprise him in my school uniform.

I can't wait till Monday. At least I think I can't, because I've suddenly remembered we've got end-of-term exams next week, so I'll probably have to spend all weekend revising, and I still haven't glued the tissue-paper onto my Hurricane.

Thursday, July 19th

I TOLD Chimp Harris that Daddy was coming back and that he would be in time for the Fathers' Match next Thursday. He seemed quite pleased, though not as pleased as all that.

When I asked him if I could play if Daddy played, he said, 'A tradition is a tradition. It is the loam and plaster that keeps the fabric of our school together.' I hope that means yes.

Friday, July 20th

I was walking through Heroes' Hall on my way to Carpentry this afternoon when I saw Raincock coming in the other direction, singing in a loud voice, 'This time next week where will I be? Not in this academee!' Luckily I didn't join in because at that moment The Chimp came out of his study. Raincock didn't see him because he was behind him, and went on singing and jumping about. The Chimp shouted, 'How many times have I told you? "Will" denotes determination, "shall" denotes future intention. I *shall* punish you . . . you *will* run round Lower Field twenty-five times after school in full batting order, including pads and box.' He gave Raincock one of his really painful head-slaps and walked off down Prior's Passage.

Saturday, July 21st

I was going to start revising History and Latin this morning, but then Colin came round after breakfast to say shall we do our aeroplanes, so I have decided to start tomorrow instead. Colin finished papering his Hurricane ages before me. I don't know why I always get glue on my fingers and he doesn't, but he just doesn't. In the end he had to finish mine off.

After lunch we painted the wings with dope. I managed to do mine quite well, though after a while I felt a bit woozy and had to go out in the garden. Mrs Penwarden gave me a glass of water and made me sit on the verandah with my head between my legs until I felt better. Colin says he felt quite woozy once when he was filling his father's cigarette lighter with petrol and thought it was quite nice. He said he had heard that drinking gin makes you feel woozy, too.

I wonder if Mummy feels woozy when she drinks gin. She talks quite loudly and laughs at jokes that aren't funny, but she usually only does that when Uncle Bob comes round to play canasta. He's not really my uncle. His real name is Captain Deighton but he said I could call him Uncle if I wanted, and Mummy said, as he's an old friend of the family, it was all right.

I asked if I could play canasta with them one evening. Uncle Bob gave her a funny look and she said it's a grown-up game, perhaps when I am older. I'd like to learn to play one day. It sounds great fun. I can hear them when I'm in bed, giggling away like mad downstairs. They used to play at least once a week, but he hasn't been round for ages. I asked Mummy when he was coming round next and she said she didn't know, everything was bound to be different now the war's over. I hope he does come again soon, then he can meet Daddy. I'm surprised he doesn't know him already, being an old friend of the family. Perhaps he's just forgotten. After all, Daddy has been away for three years.

Sunday, July 22nd

I TRIED revising semi-deponent verbs and The Pilgrimage of Grace, but I couldn't stop thinking about tomorrow and wondering if I'll be home in time to meet Daddy at the station. In the end I gave up and made a huge sign saying WELCOME HOME, DADDY instead. Mummy seemed really pleased when I showed it to her and we went up into the loft and got out a string of little Union Jacks that she and Daddy had bought for the Coronation of Edward VIII and never used and we spent the morning hanging them up over the front door with some old balloons and my sign. It looked really welcoming. I'm sure he'll be pleased.

Mummy said, 'I've got two eggs left. I'll make a little jam sponge.' I asked her if it would be as nice as vinegar cake which is what we usually have, and she said it would be much nicer. I said what about an egg for Daddy's breakfast on Tuesday? She said she'd try and scrounge one from Mrs Harrington. I feel almost as excited as I do at Christmas.

In the afternoon I went down to Colin's and we glued the engines to the stringers. Actually, I'm quite glad now I've got the 1cc model. The 2cc would be much too heavy. I bet Colin's is terribly nose-heavy. After that we put a second coat of dope on the wings. I tried holding my breath all the time, but finished up feeling even woozier than I did when I didn't.

When I got home, Mummy said that I had just missed Daddy. I thought for a mo. she meant he had come home early, but actually he'd telephoned from Liverpool to say he'd disembarked and that he had no idea when he'd be able to catch a train to London, but he'd call as soon as he arrived. I asked her if he'd shaved off his moustache. She said she couldn't tell on the telephone, but it sounded like it.

G.H. Elliott, the Chocolate-Coloured Coon, is on 'Variety Bandbox' later. I hope I'll be allowed to stay up and listen in. I don't really like him that much, but I know I won't be able to go to sleep for hours thinking about tomorrow.

Monday, July 23rd

I CAN'T remember anything that happened this morning, except that I fell asleep in the middle of Geography with my chin in my hand. My elbow must have slipped because the next thing I knew I had banged my chin really hard against the edge of my desk.

The exam timetable went up on the board in Break. I've got English I and Maths I tomorrow morning and History and French I in the afternoon, and on Wednesday I've got Latin and Geography in the morning, and Maths II and English II. I wish I had done more revision.

I went to see Matron in Break and told her what had happened in Geography. I said my chin really hurt and I felt quite dizzy and did she think I ought to be let off exams tomorrow? She asked me if I could remember what I'd had for breakfast. I said, yes, Force flakes, a rasher of bacon, toast and honey. She said, 'In that case, no.'

Games ended early and I ran most of the way home until I got to the field at the top of the road. I walked slowly down towards the house, but my heart was still beating really hard. I tiptoed round the side of the house and looked in all the windows to see if he was there. There was a huge tea on the dining room table with sandwiches and biscuits and the jam sponge in the middle. It was really peculiar seeing three places laid. Mummy was in the kitchen topping and tailing some runner beans. She said, 'Thank goodness you're here. Daddy rang to say he was catching the 4.10 from London Bridge. It should be in any minute. We'd better get our skates on.'

As we drove down to the station, my mouth felt really dry, just like it does when I have to go and stand outside Chimp Harris's door. I also felt a bit sick, but wasn't, luckily.

The 4.10 had been cancelled so we had to sit on the platform for ages until the next train came. There were lots of other people waiting, including Anthony Masterson-Smith and his mother. Anthony said, 'We've come to meet my father.' I said, 'Same here.' He said, 'What rank's your father?' I told him major. He said, 'Mine's a half-colonel.' I said, 'So what?' He said, 'Yours will have to call mine sir.' I asked him if his father had ever met Monty but before he could answer, Mummy said, 'Come along, darling,' and marched me off down the platform.

When the train finally came in, lots of people got off. Some were wearing their uniforms and carried kitbags over their shoulders but most were in hats and coats. Brown and grey, mostly. A lot of them were smoking cigarettes. Then Mummy pointed to the far end of the platform and said, 'Look, there he is!' and we started to walk along the platform. It was quite difficult pushing our way through all the people and at first I couldn't see which one he was, but then suddenly there was a gap and I recognised him.

He was taller and thinner than I expected, and very brown. Also a bit balder. He still had his moustache, though. I ran forward to meet him. He suddenly gave a big smile and I smiled back, but then he walked right past me and went up to Mummy and they hugged each other for ages. Mummy's eyes were shining. I think she was crying.

I didn't know what to do, so I just stood there and she looked at me over his shoulder and said something to him and they stopped hugging and he turned round and looked at me. I went a bit red then and didn't know what to say. But then Daddy said, 'Hallo, tadpole. Fancy you not recognising your old father!' I was going to say that actually I *had* recognised him when he said, 'Well, don't just stand there.' I went up to him and we shook hands. Mummy said, 'Aren't you going to give Daddy a kiss?' He said, 'Oh, he's too old for that sort of thing now, aren't you?' I said that I was. 'Probably too old to be called tadpole, too, eh?'

Actually, I wouldn't have minded if he had kissed me, or at least given me a hug, except that Anthony and his father were walking past at the time. I was glad Daddy wasn't in uniform

WELCOME HOME, DADDY

so he didn't have to salute him anyway. I made a rude face at Anthony but he pretended not to see me.

Daddy ruffled my hair and said, 'I hope you've been looking after your mother.' I said yes and so had Uncle Bob. He said, 'Who's Uncle Bob?' but before I could say anything more, Mummy said, 'Oh, he's one of my many cousins. You haven't met him.' Daddy said, 'I never knew you had a cousin called Bob.' Mummy said, 'He's very distant.' She never said anything to me about him being a cousin. I don't know whether to mention it or not. Best not, probably.

Mummy drove home. On the way I told Daddy about how we'd got the car started and about the girls moving in up the road and how they'd got a swimming-pool and everything, but he didn't say very much. When I asked him if he wanted to play in the Fathers' Match on Thursday, all he said was, 'We'll see.'

The flags had fallen down on one side of the door which was a shame, but I think he quite liked my WELCOME HOME sign. While Mummy was putting the kettle on he walked round the house and went into all the rooms and stood there for ages, smoking a cigarette and looking around as if he wasn't quite sure where he was. I wanted to give him my Hurricane, but Mummy said, 'After tea, perhaps. Let him get his bearings first.'

At tea he asked me how I was getting on at school, but when I began to tell him everything I'd been doing, all he said was, 'Jolly good show. Keep it up.' I was going to tell him about Stuffy Bedding throwing Holmes-Johnson out of the window in Maths, but didn't in the end.

I ate five sandwiches and three bits of cake. Jam sponge is definitely nicer than vinegar cake. Daddy didn't have any as he said he hadn't got much of an appetite. Mummy said it didn't matter, but I could see she was quite upset. I said he should try some because Mummy had used up her last egg to make it. Daddy laughed and said, 'Well, we'll just

have to buy some more then, won't we?' Mummy
and I looked at each other, but we didn't say
anything. As I was helping her to clear the table
she whispered, 'Daddy doesn't know what it's been like in
England. Don't say anything. We wouldn't want to spoil his
day.'

After tea I gave him the Hurricane. He seemed quite
pleased, even though I had made a bit of a bosh shot with the
markings. Then we went out into the garden to fly it. Luckily
I got the engine going first time. I asked Daddy if he would like
to fly it first, and he said yes, so I held on to the plane while he
picked up the control line. I called out, 'Say when.' 'Okay,' he
said, 'now.' I let go and the plane bounced across the grass and
took off. It went really well, much faster than I thought, also
much higher. Mummy shouted, 'Oh, well done, darling,' and
cheered and clapped.

I don't know what happened exactly, but the line got caught
in the tall yew tree and the plane went round and round in
smaller and smaller circles, and then suddenly the line broke
and the plane went straight up in the air for miles, and then the
engine stopped and it came hurtling down and smashed to
smithereens in the rockery. I was really fed up, but all Daddy
said was, 'Worse things happen in war,' and ruffled my hair
and took Mummy's hand and they went off indoors. I very
nearly blubbed, but I'm glad I didn't. I think the engine's OK,
but the propellor's completely bent. It's odd to think that Colin
who's twelve and a quarter can loop-the-loop with a balsa-
wood plane, but Daddy who was a Desert Rat can't get it to fly
past a tree without hitting it.

We had roast chicken for supper. After we'd finished eating,
Daddy said, 'If you look in my attaché case, you may find
something that'll interest you.' I began to say, 'Is it . . . ?' but
he said, 'Wait and see.' I put my hand in but
couldn't find anything like the shape of a pistol.
'Well?' he said. I said, 'Do you mean
this?' and pulled out something
about the size of a large stone
wrapped in newspaper. He said,
'Open it.' I did, and there *was* a stone
inside. I stared at it. He said, 'Do
you like it?' I said I wasn't sure
what it was.

He said, 'It's a scarab. It's a precious gem carved in the shape of a beetle. If you look underneath you'll see there's a design which you can press into the sealing wax on important envelopes. Everyone has them in Egypt. That one's made of amethyst. It's very, very old.' Mummy said, 'Well, what do you say?' I said, 'Thank you very much, sir.' He said, 'Please don't call me sir.' Mummy said, 'Don't worry, he does it to me all the time. He'll probably call you Matron next.' And they both laughed. I put the scarab in my pocket. It's not as good as a Mauser, but I do quite like it.

The Air Force edition of 'Merry-Go-Round' was on the wireless. When I asked Daddy if he wanted to listen in he frowned and said 'What?' I said, 'You know, the Most Famous Station in Laughter Command, Much-Binding-in-the-Marsh. Stinker Murdoch's really funny. And Kenneth Horne always says, "When I was in Sidi Barrani . . ."' Daddy said, 'I don't think I met anyone called Horne.'

Mummy said, 'I think Daddy's tired, we'll probably go to bed early,' so they did. I listened to 'Merry-Go-Round' for a bit but it didn't seem as funny as usual so I turned it off and got an apple and went to my room to read.

I tiptoed past their door, but I couldn't hear any giggling or anything. Perhaps they were asleep. Or playing canasta.

Tuesday, July 24th

FIRST day of exams. I felt so sick when I woke up that I couldn't eat any breakfast. Daddy came down in his pyjamas and dressing-gown just as I was leaving and said, 'Do your best, old man. You can't do more.' I thought, 'You can if you've done some revision,' but all I said was 'Okay', and ran out. I really love having Daddy home but it's much more difficult to talk to him than I expected. I don't suppose you meet many twelve-year-old boys when you're a Desert Rat. I expect he'll get more used to me soon. I do hope so. At the moment he talks to me in a really gruff way, like Grandpa. He smokes as much as Grandpa, too.

In English we were given a poem called 'The Way Through the Woods' by Rudyard Kipling and we had to pick out examples of different things, like a temporal clause, a conditional clause, a present participle, alliteration, onomatopoeia, etc.

Pretty peasy if you ask me. The funny thing is, there wasn't a single question about what the poem's about.

Everyone thought Maths I was really hard. One question was: 'State (but do not prove) any properties you know of a rhombus which do not apply to other parallelograms.' Wetherby-Brown wrote 'Who cares?' Everyone laughed when he told us, but I noticed he didn't have a second helping of mince at lunch.

'It's a scarab' (p. 47)

In History I wrote a page and a half about Lambert Simnel and Perkin Warbeck and two pages about The Pilgrimage of Grace, even though I hadn't revised it. I didn't remember anything like as much about The King's Great Matter, though. Wetherby-Brown thought it meant Henry VIII's fat stomach and wrote three pages about how many chickens he could eat at one go and how he used to eat them with his fingers and then throw the bones over his shoulder.

Part of the French exam was an oral. We all had to sit in the Library and Mr Warburton called us up and asked us questions in French about our school. 'How many pupils are there at your school?', 'What lesson do you enjoy?', that sort of thing. France must be a really boring place if that's all they talk about over there.

When it came to Seabrook's turn, Mr Warburton said, '*Asseyez-vous.*' Seabrook said, 'Seabrook, sir.' Mr Warburton said, '*Non, non, asseyez-vous,*' and pointed at the chair. Seabrook said, 'Seabrook, sir.' Mr Warburton frowned and said '*Asseyez-vous, asseyez-vous*' in a cross voice. This time Seabrook looked really puzzled and said, 'Seabrook, sir,' again. Mr Warburton walked across, grabbed Seabrook and pushed him into the chair and said, 'Oh, sit down, you bloody fool.' Seabrook started crying. Mr Warburton said, 'No one ever got anywhere in France by grizzling, as we discovered to our cost in 1940. Nought out of twenty.' And he pulled Seabrook out of the chair, kicked him up the bottom and chucked him out of the room.

I wanted Daddy to play cricket with me after tea, but he couldn't as he had arranged to play squash with his friend Dickie Pargeter and meet some friends afterwards for a drink at the Hoskins' Arms. He said they were all in the same outfit and they had some fat to chew over, but that he'd try and fit in a few overs later on.

He still wasn't back by nine o'clock so I put the cricket things away and went to get ready for bed. While Mummy was washing my hair I asked her whether Uncle Bob really was her cousin. She said, 'Very distant.' I said I really missed him. She said, 'So do I. He's a very nice man. He was very kind to me while Daddy was away.' I said in that case why didn't they ask him round? She said she didn't think that was a very good idea. When I asked her why, she said she didn't think Daddy and he would have much in common. I said what about canasta? She said Daddy didn't know how to play canasta. I said that Uncle Bob could teach him. She said she didn't think Daddy was in any mood to be taught new games for the time being, and that anyway Uncle Bob had gone away for a while. I asked her where and she said, 'South Africa.' I said, 'But he is coming back, isn't he? We are going to see him one day?' She said, 'I don't think so,' and ran out of the room and I had to rinse my hair and dry it myself. I went to say goodnight, but her bedroom door was shut. I thought I could hear her crying, but it may have been the owl in the wood at the bottom of the garden.

Wednesday, July 25th

WE had Latin and Geography this morning. I thought Accusative and Infinitive would probably come up and they did, so did Ablative Absolute, but there was nothing about Gerunds and Gerundives which was really unfair as Gnasher Davies had said there would be and I had revised them specially. I expect he did it on purpose to annoy us. Geography was the usual sort of thing. Coastal erosion, latitudes and longitudes, crop rotation in Tanganyika and Nyasaland, etc.

My pen ran out in the middle of Maths II and I had to go to Stationery and fill it up, so I wasn't able to finish the question about the man going up and down the escalator. I'm quite glad my pen ran out, actually, because I couldn't do it anyway. In English II I wrote three pages on 'A Day in the Life of a Threepenny Bit'. I thought it was quite good myself.

I was on my way back from Tub when somebody grabbed my ear and gave it a sharp twist. It was Chimp Harris. He said,

'Is your father going to play in the match tomorrow, Bodge, or not?' I explained that he had only arrived home from Egypt yesterday and wasn't quite sure. The Chimp said, 'Where he's arrived from and when is neither here nor there. Either he wants to play or he doesn't. If he does, let me know by eight o'clock, if he doesn't I'll ask somebody else.' He gave my ear another really sharp tweak and walked away.

I ran all the way home, but Daddy wasn't there. He had gone down to the Plumber's Arms with Dickie Pargeter to meet some Army friends. I asked Mummy when he would be back and she said that my guess was as good as hers. I told her about having to say whether he could play before eight o'clock. Mummy said, 'I'm sure he wouldn't want to miss the game if you're playing. Why don't I ring Mr Harris up and say yes?'

I waited up till nine o'clock so that I could tell Daddy, but he didn't come so I went to bed with an apple and the latest Biggles which Mummy had got out for me from the Boots Library. I was so excited about the match that I couldn't concentrate and I couldn't get to sleep either, so I knelt up and looked out of the window. It was still quite light, even though it was nearly after ten o'clock. Mr Henriksen was still mowing his lawn over the road at Tupwood and the Ballards next door at Brambles were sitting on their terrace having what they call 'one of their *soirées*' and talking French all the time, or at least trying to. They do it quite often, I don't know why. They're easily as old as Grandma and Grandpa.

Their accents are even worse than Mr Warburton's and their grammar is completely wrong. Whenever they get stuck they make it up. I heard Mr Ballard saying, '*Quoi environs un chapeau de nuit, vieux chose?*' Mrs Ballard giggled and said, '*Je ne comprender vous pas.*' Mr Ballard said, '*Quoi environs* . . . what about . . . *un chapeau de nuit* . . . a night-cap . . . *vieux chose* . . . old thing.' I thought they'd never stop laughing. They're always laughing.

Thursday, July 26th

I WOKE up at half-past five and couldn't get back to sleep, so I got up, tiptoed downstairs and went out into the garden in my pyjamas and dressing-gown. The grass was covered with dew so I took off my slippers and walked around in my bare feet. It was a really nice feeling. I suddenly started thinking about Colin's cousin Amanda and wondering when the Pardoes are thinking of filling their pool.

I tried practising a few of my off-spins, but the tennis ball got soaked, so I took my bat and hit some shots against the garage door instead. After a while the back door opened and Daddy came out. I thought he might have come to practise as well, but he said, 'Have you the foggiest idea what time it is?' I said I thought about six. He said, 'Exactly. I've just had a telephone call from Mrs Freeman next door complaining about the noise you're making. Have you no consideration for others?' I tried to explain that I was practising for the Fathers' Match. 'Oh, do stop going on about that wretched match, for goodness' sake,' he said. I said, 'You *are* playing, aren't you? Mummy rang to say you were, so that means I will be too.' Daddy said, 'She had no business doing anything of the sort without asking me first. As it happens, I've got to go up to Town after breakfast and see some people at Lloyd's.' And he sent me back up to my room. I didn't mean to cry, but I did. I really wanted to play in the match and I thought he wanted to as well. He doesn't seem to want to do anything much with me.

The Chimp grabbed me by the ear after Chapel and said, 'Thank God this country didn't have to depend on people like your father when we stood alone in 1940.' I said I was very sorry but he'd had to go up to London and see some people at Lord's. Mr Harris said, 'Badger's Mount Fathers' Match not good enough for him, eh?' And he gave my ear another sharp twist. It really hurts when he does that, though not as much as when Stuffy Bedding pulls the bit of hair in front of your ear and twiddles it round. He did that to Wetherby-Brown once and pulled a huge tuft out. When Wetherby-Brown cried, he gave him a detention.

I wanted to go home in the afternoon, but the whole school had to watch the match, which I really hated, especially as Frobisher's father was playing instead of Daddy and Frobisher got three wickets, all with worm-scarers.

The school were 45 for 4 when suddenly a Humber Hawk rolled down the bank and across the middle of the pitch. The handbrake must have slipped because there wasn't anyone in it. I thought somebody might have done something or said something, but everybody just stood and

watched it, including The Chimp and the Major who were umpiring. The only person who didn't see it was Holmes-Johnson who was at the receiving end and had his back to it. When it was about ten yards away from the wicket, The Chimp shouted, 'Wake up, Holmes-Johnson!' Holmes-Johnson suddenly turned round and saw it coming towards him, but instead of getting out of the way like the wicket keeper and all the fielders nearby, he started to run away in front of it. He looked like one of Lord Snooty's pals being chased by a bull. When he got to the other side of the pitch he kept on running and disappeared into the wood and the car went into a rhododendron bush.

Mrs Dishforth who was sitting next to Mummy and me said, 'That's the Humber for you. We bought our Armstrong Siddeley in 1938 and it's never let us down once.'

Mrs Pilbrow said, 'For my money, you can't beat a Daimler. A Royal car in every sense of the word.'

I said, 'We've got a Lanchester. It's made by the same people that make the Daimler.'

Mrs Pilbrow stared at me for a moment, then said, 'I must have a word with Ursula Gore-Andrews,' and got up and walked off.

In the end the school won by eight wickets. I bet they wouldn't have done if Daddy had been playing. At tea The Chimp came over while Mummy was queuing at the urn for a second cup and said, 'Those that sow the wind shall reap the whirlwind,' and walked off. I don't know what he was talking about and neither did Mummy. At least he didn't tweak my ear.

There were two kinds of sandwiches – pressed pig's cheek and tinned pilchards. They were both disgusting. When I told Daddy about it later, he said, 'You call that disgusting? That's nothing compared with the way the country's treated Winston. If it hadn't been for him we'd have jackboots in the Mall and the swastika flying over Buckingham Palace. And

how do we thank him? By giving him the boot. Pig's cheek and pilchards are what we deserve, and with that little twerp Attlee in charge, that's probably what we'll get.'

Friday, July 27th

Hurray! The last day of term! At breakfast Daddy said, 'Don't forget to bring back a few pots. It's time we had some silver on the sideboard.' When Mummy was kissing me goodbye she whispered, 'Don't worry, darling. There's more to life than silver cups.' Not at Badger's Mount there isn't.

After Chapel we had Cups and Prizes. Trenchard's won the House Competition, Haig's came second, Jellicoe's came third and Kitchener's came fourth. Whittington won the Warwick-Evans Cricket Cup. McGurk won the Gilfillan Athletics Trophy. Atwater's bro. won the Langrishe Diving Cup. Holmes-Johnson won the Gillespie-Smith Cup for Special Effort. I thought I might have won the Beaton Cup for the Neatest Shoe Locker, but I didn't.

After Cups and Prizes we had Marks. I hate Marks. You have to stand up in front of the whole school when your name is called out and The Chimp tells you how many marks you got out of ten for character and Major Stanford-Dingley says what the Staff think of you. Last term Wetherby-Brown got nought out of ten for funking a tackle in a 2nd XV match against Beadle Court. Mackerel-Evans got the worst mark this term – minus five out of ten for bed-wetting and moral slackness. Everyone laughed and I thought for a bit that he was going to cry, but he just rubbed his eyes and looked at the ground. I've never heard of anyone of twelve wetting their bed before.

When it came to my turn, I got five out of ten. The Major said, 'If he put as much vim into his games as he does into trying to keep out of trouble, he'd be a much more effective member of the school. He will do anything to avoid any chance of hurt or discomfort, especially in carpentry.'

Luckily Daddy was out when I got home. He seems to spend as much time away as he did during the war. When I said this to Mummy, she explained that he was probably missing his friends in the Mess, but that she was sure he would settle down to his new life soon. I hope she's right.

Saturday, July 28th

WE were in the middle of breakfast when Daddy looked out of the window and said, 'Good God, there's an Arab sheikh in the garden.' I rushed to have a look. It was Julian. You could tell it was him because real Arabs don't wear aertex shirts and grey shorts under their robes. Daddy said he would never have recognised him. I'm not surprised, dressed like that. I wanted to go out straight away, but Mummy said I had to finish my breakfast first and that Daddy had left the white of his egg specially for me. She said, 'Eggs don't grow on trees, you know.' Grown-ups say some very silly things sometimes.

In the end we called out to Julian and asked him to come in. When he did, Daddy called out, 'Park your camel outside.' Julian said, 'Sorry, sir, but that's not possible.' When Daddy asked why, Julian said, 'No palm trees.' Daddy and Mummy both roared with laughter. Julian always thinks of funny things to say, even to grown-ups. I'd never dare to talk to anyone else's father like Julian does.

Mummy said, 'Who are you meant to be, Julian? The Sheik of Araby?' Julian said, 'Lawrence of Arabia, of course.' Daddy said that, speaking as an old desert hand, he thought the outfit was very realistic, except for the flying goggles. Julian said that Lawrence was a keen motor-cyclist and that he had once seen a photograph of him on his motor bike with a pair of goggles pushed up on his forehead. 'In the desert?' I said. Julian said, 'Don't be silly. You couldn't possibly ride a motor bike in the desert. He always rode a camel, everyone knows that.' I said in that case he wouldn't have worn goggles with his robes. Julian said it's quite possible as camels can go really fast and the Arabs often have camel races.

The trouble with Julian is that he knows much more than I do about almost everything, but sometimes he makes things up so you can never really tell whether he's telling the truth or not. But it doesn't matter because I really like being friends with him. Of course I like Colin too, but he doesn't make me laugh as much as Julian. On the other hand, Julian hasn't the foggiest how to make a balsa-wood aeroplane.

Daddy asked him if he had any news of his father or his whereabouts. Julian said, 'The whole point of the Chindits is that they fight behind the Japanese lines and no one knows where they are.' Daddy said, 'Quite right, Julian. By the way, did you know that Orde Wingate, the man who founded the Chindits, never washed, he just used to brush himself?' 'Yes,' said Julian.

We couldn't go to the camp because Julian didn't want his robes to get torn, so instead we went back to his house and made a Bedouin tent using some old red curtains which we found in the lumber room. I said I thought the Bedouin always had black tents because black deflects the sun's rays. Julian said, 'Not in the north.' He always has an answer for everything. N.B. I must remember next term to ask Major Stanford-Dingley whether Lawrence wore goggles in the desert. If anyone knows, he does.

Sunday, July 29th

MUCKED about with Julian. After breakfast he came round and said why didn't we go bird's-nesting. I said I didn't want to, so we went down to the camp instead. Julian had brought his white mouse Archie with him in his trouser pocket. He let him run up and down his pullover and even in and out of his trouser-legs. I said, what if he decided to run away? Julian said, 'He may only be a mouse, but he's not completely stupid.'

Lunch at the Harringtons' was macaroni cheese and rabbit. Julian said, 'We always have macaroni cheese and rabbit. Can't we have something else for a change?' Mrs Harrington said, 'Darling heart, it really isn't as easy as you think. Meat is like gold dust these days. I'm hoping to be registered with a butcher at Broadham Green, then I'll be able to buy things like liver and kidneys.' Julian said, 'Ugh, innards,' and pretended to be sick. Mrs Harrington said, 'There are a lot of children in the world who have nothing to eat at all.' Julian said, 'I'd rather have nothing than animals' innards.' She said, 'The sooner your father comes home, the better.'

In the circumstances I was quite glad we only had rabbit for lunch, though actually I prefer spam any day.

Julian had to go to the dentist in the afternoon, so I went down to Colin's. We made a telephone with two empty cocoa tins joined together with a piece of string. Colin stood on the terrace and I stood holding the other end next to the shed on the far side of the lawn. It was quite difficult to keep the string really tight, and when we tried using thinner string, it kept snapping. But we got it going in the end and started talking to each other through it.

I could hardly hear a word he was saying, even though I pushed the tin really hard against my ear and stuck my finger in the other, but luckily Colin's got a really loud voice and I could hear him much more clearly without using the telephone at all. I wonder if Alexander Graham Bell had this sort of trouble when he started out. If he'd had Colin at the other end, he'd probably have given up altogether.

Monday, July 30th

MUMMY was in the kitchen this afternoon, smoking and listening to something on the wireless. When I asked what it was, she said, 'It's called "The Robinson Family". It's the day-to-day history of an ordinary family. There's Mr and Mrs Robinson, and Mary and Andy and Kay, and Connie and Dick. This is the first episode.'

I listened for a bit. I think it's the stupidest idea for a programme I've ever heard. For one thing it's completely boring, for another it comes on every single day. I can't understand why the BBC want to make it, or why anyone should be fagged to listen to it. If people want to know what ordinary people are doing, they can just visit their friends or relations, or stay at home.

AUGUST

Saturday, August 4th

THERE was another new programme on this evening called 'Desert Island Discs' in which Freddie Grisewood talked to someone called Roy Plomley and played eight gramophone records he would choose if he was condemned to spend the rest of his life on a desert island with a gramophone for his entertainment.

Daddy said, 'Well, that's a non-starter if ever I heard one.'

Monday, August 6th

AN amazing thing has happened. The Americans have dropped a huge bomb on Japan. Julian came round and told me. It destroyed a complete city in one go and 70,000 people were killed straight off. According to Julian, it's 2,000 times bigger than the biggest English bomb ever made, but only a tenth of the size. When I told Daddy what Julian had said, he said it sounded far-fetched to him and all that mattered was that we'd knocked the Japs for six and about time too.

But then we listened in to the news this evening and it's all true. It's called an Atomic Bomb and the explosion was equal to 20,000 tons of high explosives. According to President Truman who made a speech about it today in Washington, it harnesses all the basic powers of the universe and might be used one day as a source of power, as well as coal and oil and hydro-electricity.

That's all very well, but not if it blows up and kills 70,000 people every time it's used. The odd thing is the Japs still haven't surrendered. Daddy says they're stubborn little buggers.

Wednesday, August 8th

Aﾠccording to the news, Stalin has declared war on the Japs.
Mrs Phipps said, 'It's a bit late in the day for that.'

Thursday, August 9th

Tﾠhey've done it again. The Americans have dropped another huge bomb on another Jap city and blasted it to smithereens. Colin says it's all to do with splitting the atom and that if you split a certain sort of atom called uranium, it sets off a chain reaction which causes a massive explosion. That's why it's called an Atomic Bomb. He usually knows what he's talking about when it's anything to do with science. It's all double Dutch to me, but I still can't stop thinking about it. I also can't believe the Japs are as stubborn as all that.

On 'Children's Hour' Uncle Mac went on a flight over London in an RAF Stirling and talked about it as he went. He said the City was a very sad sight. It was really badly bombed in 1940, and other parts had been badly bombed too. Not as badly as the Jap cities, I bet.

Friday, August 10th

Wﾠhen I came in at elevenses, Mummy was going up and down with the Ewbank and listening to Oscar Rabin and his Band on 'Music While You Work'. She always seems to be listening to it when I come in. She says it just seems like that because they have it on twice a day – 10.30 in the morning on the Home Service and 3.30 on the Light Programme, as the British Forces Programme is now called.

I quite like Oscar Rabin, actually, and Felix Mendelssohn and his Hawaiian Serenaders, but I really hate Manuel and the Music of the Mountains. I don't mind Troise and his Mandoliers, though.

Sunday, August 12th

Jﾠulian came round today to say that it is the two-thousandth anniversary of Julius Caesar's invasion of Britain. Talk about stale buns. This afternoon on 'Children's Hour' they did a play called *Caesar Came to Britain* by L. du Garde Peach. Julian thought it was rather boring. I thought it was quite good, except that the Romans all spoke English which was completely wrong because they didn't speak English in England in those days, they spoke Saxon and stuff. I was wondering about writing in to Uncle Mac and telling him so. The only trouble is, he's got a really schoolmasterish voice, a bit like Stuffy Bedding's, and would probably get really batey if he was told he'd got something wrong. Still, at least he couldn't throw me out of the window.

Wednesday, August 15th

THE Japs have surrendered at last. They gave up yesterday, but it wasn't announced till late last night. Mr Attlee came on the wireless and said, 'The last of our enemies is laid low.' Daddy said that it was typical of Mr Attlee to make such a major event sound so boring. He should have been at Tub when Mr Bentham announced that Kitchener's had won the House Swimming Competition.

Mrs Harrington rang up after breakfast and said she was having a few friends round for a celebration drink on Saturday morning and would we like to go. Mummy said yes, which is really annoying. Colin and I had been planning to muck about on our bikes and now we won't be able to. Mummy said we could do that any day, which shows how much she knows.

Today is VJ Day which stands for Victory in Japan Day.

Thursday, August 16th

I WAS allowed to stay up late last night to hear the King talking on the wireless. He has a funny voice, very growly, and talks with a stammer like Mackerel-Evans. He said something like, 'The war is over. We shall all feel the consequences long after we have stopped rejoicing. From the bottom of my heart I thank everybody for what they have done.' Something like that. He was nothing like as good as Mr Churchill.

THE drinks at Mrs Harrington's were not too bad. There were lots of people there like the Penwardens, the Johnsons, the Ballards, the Masterson-Smiths, the Urquarts with Rory and Lettice, Mr Henriksen and Brigadier Williams. Mrs Pardoe brought Jill and Tessa, and Anthony Masterson-Smith went like a tomato as soon as they walked into the room.

The grown-ups were drinking things called White Ladies which Mr Henriksen poured out from a jug and looked horrible. Everyone seemed to like them, though, except for Miss Sedgwick from the Boots Library and her friend Roberta who both wore trousers and drank pale ale. Mummy says that women who have been Wrens in the war always drink beer and always wear trousers. Julian found a glass of White Lady lying around and he and Colin and Rory Urquart and I had a sip each. It was even more horrible than it looked. Mrs Pardoe got tiddly and tried to kiss Brigadier Williams. I can't imagine why. He's very old. We all tried adding extra orange to our orange squash but we couldn't get rid of the taste of the White Lady for ages.

We were having a really interesting conversation about things that make you sick when Mummy came up and said why didn't I talk to Jill Pardoe? I said I didn't want to and anyway you can't talk to girls. They don't talk about interesting things.

Mummy told me not to be silly and went off to get her. Rory said that actually Jill's quite pretty and looks like Petula Clark in *Radio Fun*. Julian said he thought she looked more like Korky the Cat in *Dandy*. Colin said, 'Well, anyway, she's not as nice as my cousin Amanda.' I said I'd quite like to meet her. Colin said, 'Well, you can't. She gone on holiday to Angmering with her parents.'

Mummy brought Jill across. I thought everyone would run away but they just stood there sniggering. I tried talking to her, but I don't know why I bothered. I told her all about Julian and me playing Chindits in the rhododendrons near the camp. I thought Julian would help me and say something, but he just stood there grinning like a baboon and kept his trap shut. Actually, Jill seemed to be quite interested, but when I had finished all she said was, did I like Princess Margaret Rose? I said I did, quite. She said, oh good, would I like to go round and look at her Royal Family scrap-book some time? I said maybe, and everyone sniggered even more.

Mrs Masterson-Smith came up with Anthony and said why didn't we all go off and play a game of hide-and-seek, so we told the girls to hide, then we got Anthony to go and look for them, and Colin and Julian and Rory and I went off on our bikes, so the day wasn't completely wasted after all.

Sunday, August 19th

WE had roast lamb for lunch. Daddy said the joint in his knee was bigger than that. Mummy said that, talking about knees, she had had to go down on hers in the butcher's to get it, and that even then it had used up nearly our whole meat ration for a month. By the time Daddy had carved it, there were only three tiny slices each. Mummy said, 'You'll have to make up for it with vegetables,' and gave me an extra potato. Daddy said, 'There's favouritism if ever I saw it.' I told him he could have it if he wanted, but Mummy said certainly not, growing bodies need every bit of goodness they can get. Daddy said, 'And mollycoddling, by the look of it.' I thought for a moment they were going to have an argument.

This afternoon Daddy went down into the cellar and got out his old golf clubs. They're called Bingham's 'Clingers' and they have funny oval shafts with white rings round the bottom. He took them out onto the terrace, got out the driver and a handful of old balls and started whacking them into the wood. The first few went off sideways into the Freemans' garden.

'Damned slice,' said Daddy and fiddled with his hands. After that they all went straight into the trees. Mummy called out, 'Do be careful, darling. You might hit someone.' Daddy said, 'Unlikely,' and hit another straight into the Freemans' garden. I thought he was going to ask if I wanted to have a go, but he went on hitting the balls until they had all gone and then said, 'Nothing much wrong with my swing after five years.' I said I'd really like to learn how to play golf and perhaps he could teach me. He said, 'One of these days, perhaps,' and put the clubs away again.

Monday, August 20th

THERE'S a man who comes on 'Children's Hour' called Nomad the Naturalist. He pretends to live in a cottage called The Look-Out and he invites listeners to visit him and talks about birds and animals and things. The programme's called At Home with Nomad. I'd rather be at home with Stuffy Bedding. At least with Stuffy quite exciting things happen.

Tuesday, August 21st

THE hottest day of the holidays so far. It was so hot I took my shirt off after breakfast and went down and sat in the camp to cool off. While I was there I found this amazing caterpillar. It's about three inches long with dark brown bristles and has a brilliant green tuft like the Grand Vizier in *The Thief of Baghdad*, except on its tail. I took it home and put it in a jam

jar with holes in the top and gave it some leaves to eat. It seems quite happy in there, though it's difficult to tell whether a caterpillar is happy or not. Anyway, it has curled up in a ball and gone to sleep. Mrs Phipps said I should have left it where it was, but I think if I had done, it could easily have been eaten by a bird or run over by the motor mower. She said, 'It's a caterpillar's fate.' I said, 'Not this one's.'

I was in the middle of listening to Howard Marshall commentating on the Third Test at Old Trafford when Julian came round. I showed him my caterpillar, but he wasn't interested at all. He has just come back from staying with the Goodmans in Bromley. A chauffeur came to collect him in a huge American car with a cocktail cabinet in the back. Julian said the beds were the plushest he had ever seen and the lavatory seat had a pink woolly cover and when you sat on it, it played 'The More We Are Together'.

Thursday, August 23rd

COLIN came round and we spent the whole morning experimenting with the home-made telephone. In the end we were able to speak to each other from the vegetable garden to the terrace without raising our voices at all. Then Colin stayed for lunch. Mummy made cabbage cheese. She said it made a nice change from cauliflower, but it didn't.

The telephone rang in the middle of lunch. It was Mrs Freeman from next door, saying that her wireless set had been crackling all morning and would we stop using our telephone near her house. Mummy said it couldn't have been our fault as it's only made out of string and cocoa tins, but Mrs Freeman said that any fool knows that sound waves interfere with wireless sets. How else do voices come out of them in the first place? Anyway, if we didn't put a stop to it immediately, she'd be ringing up the police.

Friday, August 24th

NOTHING much has happened this week, except the leather on my bicycle saddle has completely worn out and the sharp bit on the end of one of the springs came through and tore a hole in my grey shorts. I'm really glad. They were my cousin Denis's and he passed them on to me. They're bristly and they have a funny smell. Mummy said, never mind, she could easily put a darn in them. When she wasn't looking, I got them out of her needlework cupboard and tore them even more. I don't think I'll be having to put up with that smell for much longer. I'm trying to think of a way of doing the same thing to Denis's old aertex shirts, and his socks.

Saturday, August 25th

TODAY has been even hotter. I slept all night without my pyjama jacket, and just a sheet. The milk at breakfast was quite warm, even though it had been in the meat safe all night. Mummy said that in America all families have fridges for keeping food fresh and cold and it's a pity we don't have them here. Daddy said, 'They have gangsters with tommy-guns in America, but that doesn't mean we want them rampaging up and down Station Road East, and filling the gutters of Chichele Road with blood.'

In the afternoon we went to watch Daddy play cricket for

Limpsfield against Moorhouse. It's the first time he's played since the beginning of the war. 'I warned them I was as rusty as hell,' he said.

Mummy said, 'Darling, it's only a local club match. You're not being asked to open for England against Australia.' Daddy said, 'It feels like it.'

On the way there, we saw a man standing at a bus stop. He was wearing a blazer with a large crest on the breast pocket and there was a cricket bag on the ground beside him. I said, 'Can we give him a lift?' Daddy said, 'I don't think so.' I said, 'He might be playing in the same game as you.' Daddy said, 'It's possible, but I think he'd be happier taking the bus.' I said, 'But what if the bus doesn't come?' Daddy said, 'Buses always come in the country. It's one of the reasons we moved to Surrey.'

We parked the car in the road and climbed through the bracken to the Moorhouse cricket ground up on the hill. I carried Daddy's cricket bag. I was quite puffed out when I got there. There wasn't a pavilion, just a black shed. I put the bag inside while he went off to talk to the Limpsfield captain. Some of the players were already in there, smoking Woodbines and rummaging in their bags and pulling out crumpled white trousers. It was so pongy I had to hold my breath.

The man we saw at the bus stop arrived about ten minutes later. He was very red in the face and sweating a lot. The badge on his blazer was even bigger than I thought, and very wiry. Also he had a very thin moustache, a bit like Arthur English. When I told Daddy he was there, he said, 'What did I tell you? We may not be able to get a good steak for love or money, but at least the buses still run on time.' Mummy said, 'I still think we could have given him a lift.' Daddy said, 'Other ranks prefer to make their own travel arrangements.'

Moorhouse batted first. One of their opening batsmen wore a cap with a tiny peak which was flat on his forehead and ended up on the bridge of his nose. He had a little moustache and looked like a sergeant-major in a book I've got on the Boer War. He only ever played one shot which was sweeping the ball to leg. When he made contact the ball went for miles, but mostly it hit the top edge of the bat and flew up in the air. No one could catch it because it was impossible to tell where it was going to go, and no one could stop the ball either because the outfield was so full of holes and ridges that even if you got right behind the ball it would still shoot past you at the last minute. The Moorhouse captain said that was because it was used at the beginning of the war as a tank training ground.

In the end the sergeant-major hit one really hard that went miles over mid-wicket's head and when it hit the ground it shot straight back towards the wicket and was caught by the leg slip, who ran him out.

Moorhouse were all out in the end for 142. There was a huge tea which the wives and girl-friends had carried up in baskets. I had four paste sandwiches and three flapjacks and three glasses of orange squash. I felt a bit sick afterwards.

Limpsfield started off quite well and were 68 for two when Daddy went in. He batted much better than anyone else and hit some beautiful off-drives. He was on 48 when he was bowled by the biggest leg break I've ever seen.It landed about two feet outside the leg stump and knocked out the off stump. Daddy just laughed when he came out and said, 'We could use a bowler like that against Australia.'

Then the man we'd seen at the bus stop was put on to bowl. He's called Brylcreem Bradshaw. His trousers were covered with green stains and his cricket boots were tied with string. His hair was plastered so flat on his head it looked as if it had been painted on. Even when he was bowling flat out, it never moved. They once showed Keith Miller bowling against England on the *Topical Budget* at the Plaza and Brylcreem Bradshaw was easily as fast as him, but much more dangerous. Sometimes the ball kept low, sometimes it whizzed past at head height.

One of the Limpsfield batsmen played forward to a well pitched-up ball that never bounced at all. It went straight under his bat and knocked out his middle stump. When he came in, he said, 'I thought Monte Cassino was bad, but that was nothing compared with what I've just been through.'

In the end Limpsfield were all out for 102. Brylcreem Bradshaw took 6 for 28.

Afterwards everyone went down to the Grasshopper. Another boy and I played cricket in the car park and every now and then someone came out and gave us some Tizer. I really like Tizer. It's fizzy and much sweeter than the drinks we have usually. I wish we had it all the time instead of orange squash, which doesn't taste of anything much and is always rather sour.

It was almost dark by the time we left. Daddy and Mummy were both very merry. As we were reversing out of the car park we bumped into a lamp-post. Daddy said, 'It was driving far too fast and on the wrong side of the road.' I've never heard Mummy laugh so much. Daddy made lots of funny jokes in the car in a voice like Monty, about knocking Moorhouse for six right out of Kent.

I wish he joked like that all the time.

Sunday, August 26th

WHEN I came in at elevenses, Mummy said that Mrs Pardoe had rung to say they've filled the swimming-pool and would I like to go round after lunch and bathe. I said I couldn't. Mummy said, 'But I've said you'd like to go. Barbara Kippax is going, and Anthony Masterson-Smith.'

The real reason I didn't want to go was because I can't swim properly yet and I didn't want anyone to find out, especially Anthony Masterson-Smith, and I knew that Mummy would say it didn't matter and that I could stay in the shallow end and no one would notice, so instead I said that actually I wasn't feeling very well. Mummy said, 'In that case you'd better go up to your room and stay there for the rest of the day.'

I said could Colin come round and help me mend my Hurricane? Mummy said that Colin was going to the Pardoes' as well and so was his cousin Amanda who was staying. I said that Colin told me she was on holiday in Angmering. Mummy said, 'Well, she's obviously come back because she's staying with the Penwardens and is going with Colin to the Pardoes' this afternoon.'

I said that when I said I wasn't feeling very well, it was a slip of the tongue and what I really meant was that I *hadn't been* feeling very well, but that I was beginning to feel much better and I was sure that I would have completely recovered by lunchtime. She said it was better to be safe than sorry and that a quiet day in my room with a book wouldn't do me any harm at all.

I'm in my room now, actually, and I can hear people laughing and shouting and the sound of splashing water coming from Meadowcroft. I don't expect anyone is actually bathing bare, but even so I can't help wondering. I wasn't feeling at all unwell earlier, but I jolly well am now.

Never mind, I expect Mrs Freeman will soon put a stop to the fun.

(Later: she did.)

Monday, August 27th

Mummy came back from shopping in Oxted and said there's going to be even more rationing and food shortages. I thought everything was going to get better and there'd be lots more to eat and no more food that tastes completely disgusting, like vinegar cake and bright green jelly made without sugar, and horse meat with lumps of yellow fat hanging off it, and casseroled whale meat, and braised heart. What's the point of winning the war otherwise? Mrs Phipps says things are worse now than they were when the war was on, and I agree.

No one seems to be very happy. Mummy and Daddy don't, anyway. Daddy spends hours alone in the garden, mowing the lawn or fiddling about in the potting shed, and when he isn't doing that he's out at the pub with Dickie Pargeter and his Army pals. He never gets home from work until after I've gone to bed, which is 8.30 usually. Sometimes he comes in so late I don't ever hear him. He seems very cross nearly all the time and didn't seem to be at all interested when I told him about my saddle. In fact, he doesn't seem to be interested in anything much I do or tell him. I always thought fathers were supposed to take an interest in what their children do. The trouble is, I haven't had one for ages and the boys at school never talk about their parents. In fact, the only boy I know who ever talks about his father is Anthony Masterson-Smith, and he only does it to swank.

Anyway, something isn't quite right, and when I asked Mummy what the matter was, she said it was nothing to worry about. It isn't easy getting back into the swing of things, I know. I have the same problem at the beginning of every term. Perhaps I should tell Daddy. It might help him to know that he's not the only one, but as I never see him, I never get the chance.

Mummy drinks gin a lot and stares out of the window in a moony sort of way. The other day I asked her if she was glad that Daddy was home and she said, 'I don't know,' and then she said very quickly, 'Don't be silly, of course I am,' and then she burst into tears and ran from the room.

Next time I go down to Brock's, I'll see if they've got a book on how to play canasta.

There was a talk on 'Children's Hour' this afternoon by Lieutenant-Commander R.T. Gould ('Stargazer') on The Great Waterfalls of the World. It was more interesting than I'd expected.

Tuesday, August 28th

MY report arrived this morning, worst luck. I came first in Latin, third in French, fifth in History, seventh equal in English, sixteenth in Geography, and eighteenth in Maths. Stuffy Bedding said, 'He is not a stupid boy but evidently derives great pleasure from seeming to be so. As I have told him repeatedly, he will have to pull his socks up or I can see ructions ahead.'

For History Mr Wolf put, 'I like his enquiring turn of mind but sometimes he rather overdoes it. He shows an unhealthy interest in ladies and gentlemen who lose their heads. This should be curbed at all costs.'

Geography: 'Can be fairly bright if he chooses but apparently he did not choose this term as he finished sixteenth out of eighteen. On the other hand, his stint as chalk and board-duster monitor was beyond reproach.'

English: 'Rather prone to asking stupid questions in order to raise a laugh. A bit more thought and imagination and a bit less playing to the gallery would pay dividends.'

Latin was the best. Gnasher said, 'Another excellent term's work, though he is still too often defeated by gerunds and gerundives.'

The Headmaster's report said, 'Not a bad term, though I'd like to see him enter a bit more into the rough and tumble of school life instead of cleverly avoiding any chance of hurt or discomfort. He certainly gives no trouble, but I am not sure that this is really a good thing. A little more vim in his cricket would not go amiss. His fielding is woefully bad. A happy summer holiday to you all.'

Mummy and Daddy seemed quite pleased with the report, though I had to spend ages explaining what gerunds and gerundives are. The trouble is, I don't really know the difference myself.

A talk by Dusty McGarry 'Manchester Lad' on 'Children's Hour' about his experiences with the Eighth Army was *less* interesting than I'd expected.

Wednesday, August 29th

IT says in the *Daily Express* that a whole lot of Nazis are going to be put on trial for war crimes. I don't quite understand what that means. Apparently quite a few have escaped, but Goering didn't, and he and Hess are going to be tried. Mummy said it serves them right.

Mrs Freeman rang up this afternoon to complain about the crackling on her wireless again. Mummy said that proved it couldn't have been the home-made telephone as we were in the Penwardens' garden all afternoon and that's at the other end of the road. Mrs Freeman said, 'Any half-wit knows that sound waves travel,' and put the phone down. Mummy said, 'The way she's going, she'll finish up in Nüremberg with Goering and Hess.'

Thursday, August 30th

I THOUGHT the caterpillar had escaped this morning, but it was hiding inside a curled-up leaf.

Friday, August 31st

I WAS cycling along Station Road West this morning when I saw Uncle Bob coming out of the Hoskins' Arms. I was on the point of calling out but was so surprised to see him that I didn't. By the time I'd braked and turned round he had completely disappeared. I rode up and down for a bit and looked in all the shops but I couldn't find him, so I gave up and went home.

When I told Mummy, she went rather pink and said I must have mistaken him for someone else. I said I was sure it was him and that perhaps he had come back from South Africa sooner than expected. 'Perhaps,' was all she said. I thought she would have been a bit more surprised. I also thought she would have been a bit more excited, but it seemed as if she couldn't care less. I'm quite glad now that I didn't call out when I saw him. If I do see him again, I think I'll pretend I haven't.

SEPTEMBER

Saturday, September 1st

COLIN and Julian and I were in Staffhurst Wood on our bikes and we found this old wooden hut. The door was open, so we went in and there were all these boxes full of bullets. We wondered what to do with them. I said I thought we ought to leave them where they were and tell someone, but Julian wanted to take some of them back to the camp. Colin said what for, none of us have got a gun. I said I bet my father brought his revolver home with him. Colin said, even if he had and even if we were able to get hold of it, the bullets probably wouldn't fit. Julian said that didn't matter, we could take the tips out, collect the gunpowder, and put it into old tins and make bombs with it. I said how would we set them off and Julian said, 'With a match, how do you think?' Colin said, 'They're not fireworks, you know,' and explained how you have to have a proper fuse.

In the end we decided we couldn't be fagged, so we took one bullet each just for fun and bicycled home extra fast in case someone had seen us.

Sunday, September 2nd

I PUT my bullet in the tool kit in my saddlebag, but when I tried to go to sleep last night, I kept thinking that there might be an escaped Nazi in Oxted and that he might hide in our shed and find my bullet and and put it in his gun and come and shoot one of us. I thought of getting up and going down and getting the bullet, but I was too frightened. I was too frightened to go to sleep, either, and I lay awake for hours until I heard Mummy and Daddy shouting at each other in the kitchen. I think it might have had something to do with Uncle Bob, but I couldn't really tell properly because I pulled the bedclothes over my head. Anyway, the noise would have been enough to put off any escaped Nazi and very soon afterwards I fell fast asleep. They're very tiring, the summer holidays.

Monday, September 3rd

Yesterday the Japs officially surrendered to General Mac-Arthur on a battleship in Tokyo Bay. It seems to have taken them an awful long time, considering they gave up in the middle of August. Even odder is that Julian and his mother still haven't heard a word from Colonel Harrington. I hope he's all right. Julian doesn't seem very worried, though. When I said that to Mummy, she said, 'Knowing Julian, he probably revels in the mystery.'

Wednesday, September 5th

I went to look at the caterpillar this morning for the first time in ages and he has turned himself into a chrysalis. He has attached himself to a little pad of silk on a piece of stick and has tied a silk thread round himself to stop himself falling off. I'm sorry he's not a caterpillar any more. I was getting to like him, and although a chrysalis is quite interesting, it's difficult to like it in the same way.

Thursday, September 6th

I cycled up to Hoofprints to play with Anthony Masterson-Smith. He's such a show-off. He asked me if Daddy was going to go on calling himself Major Hodge now the war's over. I asked him what else he should call himself. '*Mr* Hodge, of course,' he said. I asked him if his father was going to call himself *Mr* Masterson-Smith.' He said, 'Of course not. My father's a regular soldier and his rank is a real rank. Your father's is only substantive.' When I asked him what that meant, he said, 'Don't you know anything? It means your father's is only a wartime rank and now the war's over he has to give it up and become just an ordinary person again.' I said, so what? He said, so nothing, he was just telling me, that's all. I said, 'Well, I've got something to tell you. Jill Pardoe's coming round later.' It wasn't true but I wanted to see if he would go red and he did, straight away. Good.

For lunch we had vegetable pie which looked exactly like sick, and tasted like it too. After that we had something called Shape which looked like pale green blancmange in the shape of the letter *s* and tasted of pale green nothing. Mrs Masterson-Smith asked me if I liked it and I said yes, although actually it had lumps in it, like sick, and I very nearly *was* sick every time I swallowed some. When I asked her what it was, Mrs Masterson-Smith said it was just the same as real blancmange except using saccharine instead of sugar. It was Anthony's favourite. It would be.

Mrs Masterson-Smith was wearing a skirt which was all furry and in different shades of yellow. It looked exactly like a lot of old dusters sewn together, but I didn't say anything. When I told Anthony afterwards that I liked his mother's skirt, he said, 'Yes, it is nice, isn't it? She bought it from Swan and Edgar before the war. It was very expensive.'

I said, 'The funny thing is, it looks just like a lot of old dusters sewn together.' Anthony said, 'Well, that just shows how much *you* know.'

The really annoying thing is I don't know how to find out whether he's telling the truth or not.

Anyway, I couldn't care less. In my opinion, anyone's father who was a Desert Rat and knows Monty deserves to keep his rank, whether he was a regular or not.

Saturday, September 8th

THERE was another new programme on the wireless this evening called 'In Town Tonight'. It started off with the noise of traffic roaring along, and a voice shouting 'In Town Tonight . . . In Town Tonight . . . In Town Tonight . . .!' Then the voice shouted 'Stop!' and the noise stopped and the voice said, 'Once again we stop the mighty roar of London's traffic and from the great crowds we bring to the microphone some of the interesting people who are in . . . town . . . tonight!' And then someone called Flight Lieutenant Roy Rich came on and did interviews with a whole lot of people I've never heard of who weren't at all interesting.

Thursday, September 13th

I'VE suddenly realised we go back to school a week on Monday. The holidays have gone really quickly and we haven't done anything much except muck about on our bikes and play cricket in the garden and sit in the camp reading *Radio Fun*. Every time we ask one of our parents if we can go somewhere they say they haven't got enough petrol coupons. It's been really hot and it would be nice to go to the seaside and have a swim. Once we ran around in our bathing costumes all day and sprayed each other with the hose, but I burnt my shoulders in the sun and Mummy had to put calamine all over them in the evening which didn't do any good at all and I couldn't turn over in bed and had to sleep on my front, which I hate.

Mrs Pardoe said we could swim in their pool any time we wanted, but the only time we went, Jill had a whole lot of her friends from school over for the day and all they talked about was ponies and people they knew at school, and then Jill got out her scrap-book of pictures of Princess Margaret Rose, so I had to pretend I was supposed to be doing something else and went off on my bike. I didn't even put my costume on.

Rory Urquart's right. Jill does look quite like Petula Clark, but that doesn't mean I want to be friends with her. I wouldn't mind going round for a swim one day, but obviously I couldn't do it while Colin and Julian are around, and they might easily find out if I did. The other thing is, I'm not that interested in Princess Margaret Rose and don't want to look at pictures of her. If you ask me, Princess Elizabeth is much prettier. Not that I could care less. They're both much older than me, and I don't think I'm going to get married when I grow up anyway. Not if it means having rows with someone all the time.

Anyway, the man who is the chairman of the American team in 'Transatlantic Quiz' who's called Alistair Cooke gave a talk this evening called 'American Commentary'. Although he's an American, he hardly has any accent at all. Mummy says that's because he was born in England and only went to

America about fifteen years ago. I can't remember what he talked about, but I really liked listening to his voice. I wonder if he'll come on again.

There was a Paul Temple adventure on earlier called 'Send for Paul Temple Again'. I'd really like to be someone like that when I grow up. When Mummy said did I mean the actor or the man he plays, I wasn't quite sure which I meant. It's funny him having a wife called Steve. If you didn't know you might think it was a man, but of course that would be completely impossible.

Sunday, September 16th

DICKIE Pargeter called in for a drink this evening. He said there was a big reunion up at Biggin Hill yesterday to commemorate the fifth anniversary of the Battle of Britain. Apparently one of the pilots turned up at a pub in Westerham on Friday evening and asked for a room for the night. The landlord said he hadn't got a room for someone staying only one night. The pilot told him if it hadn't been for him and his friends the landlord wouldn't be there at all and threw him down the stairs.

Monday, September 17th

LORD Haw-Haw is going to be tried today. Daddy says there is no worse crime than betraying your country in time of war and that the trial is only a formality. He is sure to be found guilty and hanged.

At lunch we had macaroni cheese – *again*. Mummy gave me far too much but I wasn't allowed to leave any, so I pretended I wanted some more of the dark brown stuff on the top and took my plate out into the kitchen and scraped what was on my plate into the binette. When I came back I pretended I had eaten it all. When Mummy went out to get the stewed apples she must have opened the binette and found the macaroni because she came back holding my plate with the stuff I'd thrown away on it and made me eat it. Daddy said, 'It's not the waste that matters so much as the deception. This is exactly how children turn into people like Lord Haw-Haw.'

When I told Julian later, he said pretending to finish up your macaroni cheese had nothing to do with it. Lord Haw-Haw was Irish and that explained everything. He said it in such a definite way that it sounded as if it must be true. Daddy says he'll probably become a cabinet minister one day. It would be nice to know someone important one day. Holmes-Johnson's aunt knows Flora Robson and she stays with them sometimes.

Wednesday, September 19th

WHEN I came down to breakfast at eight o'clock this morning, Daddy was still sitting there in his pyjamas and dressing-gown, smoking. When I asked if he was going up to London as usual, he said, 'I thought I'd give it a miss today.'

Mummy came in at that moment and said that Daddy had some good news to tell me. When I asked him what, he said, 'I've got a job at Lloyd's. What do you think about that?' I said I thought he had a job already, which was why he went up to London every day. He explained he did have a job before the war, but then while he was away some frightful swine who had got out of being in the services had nabbed it. Mummy said, 'That's one reason Daddy's been a bit irritable lately.' I asked what the other reason was. She said, 'Never mind about that now. The point is, it's taken a long time and a lot of hard work, but he's back in business again at last.' Daddy said, 'It's not quite the same job as before. It's like the old one, but not so well paid, which means we'll have to tighten our belts for a while until things get going again.'

I said, 'Does that mean you won't be shouting at each other any more?' Mummy said she hoped so and Daddy nodded. I ran over to him to give him a hug. He laughed and said, 'Steady the Buffs,' and we shook hands which was nearly the same thing. Mummy gave me a hug, though.

Daddy said, 'Have you got anything special on today?' I said only that we were thinking of going dirt-tracking on our bikes up on the Common. He said, 'What would you say to a day on the beach instead? I thought we might run down to the coast and have a swim and a picnic to celebrate.'

I thought he must be joking, but when I looked at Mummy she smiled and said, 'Well?' I said could Colin and Julian come too, and she said why didn't I go and ask them.

Julian said, 'Your father must be important if he can get enough petrol coupons to drive all that way.' I said, 'He is.' He and Colin were both allowed to come, so Mummy made a lot of sandwiches – paste and sandwich spread for lunch and jam for tea – and at half-past nine we set off for Pevensey Bay.

We had good fun saluting all the AA men on their motor bikes, who saluted back, though funnily enough when we got a puncture near Uckfield and had to stop and change the wheel, we didn't see one at all. In the end it took ages to get there, about two and a half hours, and just as we arrived the sun went behind some huge clouds, so it was really cold bathing.

Colin had brought an old inner tube from a car tyre which we blew up with the foot pump from the boot. Julian had brought a blue rubber mattress with palm trees on it, plus a special little hand pump. I had never seen anything like it before. Julian said, 'My parents bought it in Juan-les-Pins before the war.' I said, 'Where's that?' He said, 'The French Riviera, of course.' I am none the wiser.

Unfortunately, Mummy got out my Mickey Mouse water rings before I could stop her, but I don't think either of the other two noticed. In fact the tide was out and the water only came up to just above our knees and anyway the others gave me turns on their things, so I didn't need anything. We stayed in for ages and the skin on my hands went all white and wrinkly.

Mummy put on her costume which was pink and had a little skirt round the bottom, but she didn't bathe. Daddy did, though. He was completely white except for his arms and the bits round his knees, which were dark brown. He looked as if he had covered them with make-up. He's even thinner than me. I thought, if we tighten our belts any further they'll meet at the back. Still, he looked really happy for the first time in ages. So did Mummy.

He wore a pair of dirty old plimsolls with holes in them when he bathed, which was just as well as Pevensey Bay beach is all pebbles. I wished I had because I suddenly felt a sharp pain in my foot and when I lifted it up to have a look there was a large crab hanging from my big toe. It was just like a cartoon from *Dandy* or *Beano*. It wouldn't let go for ages. Everybody laughed, but it jolly well hurt.

Even though it was terribly shallow, Daddy dived in and swam up and down using a funny stroke which he called a trudgeon. Mr Bentham would definitely have had something to say about it if he'd done it in Tub.

It was rather windy when we got out, so we sat under a breakwater to eat our lunch. Julian had brought some sandwiches as well which tasted really peculiar. When I asked what was in them he said, 'Dressed crab'. Daddy said, 'What was it wearing, a three-piece suit and a bow tie?' and he and Mummy laughed. Julian said that crabs didn't wear clothes and that 'dressed' meant it had been specially prepared for eating. Daddy said, 'Well done, Julian. Only trying to catch you out.' 'I realised that,' said Julian.

The sun came out after lunch. Mummy and Daddy snoozed under a blanket and we went off to look for shells, etc. Julian found a huge long piece of dark brown seaweed which he said he was going to take back to school so he could tell what the weather was going to be like. According to him, if it's going to rain the seaweed goes damp and floppy and if it's going to be fine and sunny, it goes stiff and dry. Colin said that it only went damp when it was actually raining, so it was absolutely useless for weather forecasting. Julian said he was going to take it anyway, and did.

I found a really interesting pebble. It's brownish-red and when you hold it up to the sun, the light shines right through it. Julian said it was a piece of amber, but Colin said that according to his *Wonder Book of Nature* amber was the same colour as honey and much lighter than a stone. That was because it wasn't a stone at all, it was resin that had dripped down from pine trees hundreds of thousands of years ago and had gone hard by being buried in the ground. He said you can usually tell amber because it's got a dead fly in it. Julian said if it wasn't amber, what was it? Colin said he didn't know, but it wasn't amber. Julian didn't say any more about it because he's no good at science and Colin is. I may ask one of the masters at school if he knows what it is, but it'll probably be a waste of time. Most of them know less about science than Julian.

On the way back Colin found a dried cuttlefish bone, I found three razor shells and a dead starfish and Julian stubbed his toe on something sharp that was sticking out of the sand and made it bleed, and Mummy had to put Germolene on it. He said he was sure it was part of an unexploded bomb. Daddy came to have a look, but when we dug it out it was only a rusty old bit of metal. In fact the whole beach is full of lumps of metal sticking out. Daddy says they were put there in case the Germans invaded in 1940. Julian said, 'A few lumps of metal wouldn't have been much use against the might of Hitler's panzer divisions.' Daddy said, 'They'd have been better than nothing.'

The sun had gone in again when we got back to the breakwater, but we had another dip anyway. It was absolutely freezing. My woollen bathing costume was hanging down so far when I got out that it rubbed against the insides of my knees when I walked up the beach. I tried to get dry but my towel was still damp from the morning and covered with sand which got stuck all over me, especially between my legs, and made it really uncomfortable to walk. It had got into the jam sandwiches, too, so that they were all crunchy. We ate them, though.

It took ages to pack everything up and by the time we got back to the car it was beginning to rain. Mummy got rather batey with us when we put our feet on the back seat and got sand all over it. She got even batier when she discovered I'd got tar on my shorts. The car wouldn't start, so Daddy had to get out the starting handle and crank it, and he got batey as well.

As we were driving along the road from Forest Row to East Grinstead, a policeman stepped out from the side of the road and waved us down. Then another one appeared from nowhere. Daddy said, 'What's the problem, officer?' The first policeman said, 'Would you mind stepping out of the car for a moment, sir?' Daddy asked why. The policeman said, 'If you wouldn't mind, sir.' Daddy said he *would* mind, but he got out anyway. The policeman said, 'Is this your car, sir?' Daddy said of course it was, did he look like the sort of person who went round stealing other people's cars? The policeman said, 'No offence, sir. Just a formality.' Then the second policeman got out a long glass tube with a rubber ball on the end and stuck it in the petrol tank and drew some petrol out. He examined it for a bit and then said, 'Are you aware, sir, that you are driving on red petrol?' Daddy said, 'I have no idea what you're talking about.' The policeman said, 'Someone has been selling you commercial petrol. We can tell that because all commercial petrol has a red dye in it.' Daddy said, 'What's wrong with using commercial petrol?' The policeman said, 'It is an offence in law for a private car owner to drive using commercial petrol and renders you liable to a summons.'

Mummy said, 'It's all my fault, officer. I should have warned my husband. He's only just got back from North Africa.' The policeman said, 'Oh, really, sir?' I said, 'He was a Desert Rat.' The policeman said, 'Indeed, sir?' I said, 'He was Monty's right-hand man.'

The first policeman was very interested and said that his brother had been a Desert Rat and had been killed at Alamein. Perhaps Daddy had come across him? Nobby Clark? Daddy said he was very sorry, but he hadn't. The policeman and Daddy then had a long talk about the Desert Campaign and the Eighth Army and Monty, and in the end the policeman said it had been a privilege to talk to Daddy and that in future he should take care what petrol he bought. Daddy thanked him and said he certainly would. The policeman held the car door open to let Daddy back in and then he stepped back and saluted as we drove away.

Julian said, 'Well done, sir!'

Mummy said, 'Did you know it was red petrol?' Daddy said, 'Certainly not,' and pulled a funny face. He thought we hadn't seen, but we had.

We sang all the way home. Daddy sang some rather rude music-hall songs, Mummy sang 'Lily Marlene' and 'I Couldn't Sleep a Wink Last Night', and Julian and I sang 'Mairzy Doats and Dozy Doats' but we forgot the words and we all had to go 'La la la'.

I shall definitely write about today when I do my essay on 'The Best Thing I Did in the Holidays.'

That reminds me. Only four days to go.

Thursday, September 20th

ONLY three left to go. At least I'm not a boarder, thank goodness.

'ITMA' was on this evening. They've completely changed it. Tommy Handley is now the new governor of an island called Tomtopia and he's on his way there on an ocean liner. Mrs Mopp's not in it any more, nor is Signor So-So, or The Diver, but there are lots of new characters, like Poppy Poopah, Lady Sonely and Mark Time, and a stowaway in the dining room called George Gorge who's always eating.

There was quite a funny bit when he said, 'I've had six plates of porridge, a pork chop, three plates of fat bacon, lashings of waffles and maple syrup, and a gallon of coffee. Lovely grub, lovely grub,' and Tommy said, 'What, no toast and marmalade?' The food was cooked by someone called Kurly Kale.

Friday, September 21st

ONLY two days left. This afternoon Mummy made me bicycle to Limpsfield to have my hair cut by Mr Ellis. I don't understand why a greengrocer should be any good at cutting hair, but then Mr Ellis isn't. When I complained, Mummy said, 'You can't expect salon service for 1s 3d.' Perhaps not, but I bet she wouldn't like to go back to school looking like a turnip.

After that she took me to the dentist. I had to have two fillings. Being drilled by Mr Mason was even more painful than having my toe pinched by a crab, plus it went on for much longer. You'd think by now he could afford an electric drill, instead of an ancient machine which works with a foot-pedal. It's not too bad when it first goes in, but the further in it goes, the slower he pedals and the slower the drill goes round. The noise and the vibration were almost worse than the pain. Once I almost leapt out of the chair. Mr Mason said, 'That'll be the nerve.' I asked if I could have an injection. He said, 'What does a big boy like you want with an injection?' and went on drilling.

When he'd finished, he told me I had far too many teeth in my head and that I might have to wear a plate with a brace to make them all fit in. I wouldn't mind if it was like Dishforth's. He can push his in and out just by using his tongue. He does it all the time while Mr Reader is reading poems to us like 'Young Lochinvar' and 'The Lay of the Last Minstrel' and it makes a really strange noise, somewhere between a sucking and a clicking. So does Mr Reader.

Saturday, September 22nd

ONLY one more day to go. Julian goes back to his school tomorrow and he still hasn't had any news about his father. I feel really sorry for him. I didn't at the beginning of the holidays, but now that Daddy has got his job back and he and Mummy have stopped shouting at each other, I do.

We had a last bike ride on the Common, but I got a puncture while we were dirt-tracking and we had to come home. I hate the end of the holidays, except this afternoon Daddy let me use the motor mower for the first time. I was really surprised because I didn't ask or anything. He just suddenly said, did I want to do something useful, and I said yes. It's very easy. You start it by kicking down a pedal, then you let the clutch in and off it goes. If you push the throttle lever as far as it will go, you almost have to run to catch up with it. I pretended I was driving a car. The best bit is seeing how near you can get to the herbaceous border before you pull the clutch handle up and put it out of gear. When Colin's brother Rupert cuts their lawn he doesn't bother to stop. He just goes straight across the flower bed and carries on on the other side. No one ever says anything. Rupert's leaving school in two years. I wish *I* was.

As a reward for cutting the grass, Daddy and Mummy took me and Julian to the Plaza in Oxted to see a film called *Painted Boats*. It's about these two families who live on canal boats – the Smiths and the Stoners. The Stoners are go-ahead and their boat has a motor, but the Smiths are old-fashioned and theirs is pulled by a horse. I thought it was going to end with both of them having a battle, but all that happened was that a girl in one family married a boy in the other and everyone was friends. It was pretty feeble in my view and I could see that Julian thought so too. Luckily it was jolly short, being just over an hour. But we both said how much we enjoyed it anyway. Mummy said she thought it was really nice to have a story about people getting on together and she looked at Daddy in a meaning sort of way. All Daddy said was that it moved about as quickly as the canal.

Julian said afterwards, 'Your father's quite funny.' I was rather pleased and asked him if his was, too. He said, 'How would I know?'

Sunday, September 23rd

I'M not feeling at all well. Mummy said it's probably just nerves. I asked her if I really have to go back to school tomorrow. She said, 'We'll see.' I'm not sure if I feel better or worse now.

Monday, September 24th

I'M feeling worse, but Mummy said I had to go back to school anyway. Colin and I went together on our bikes. It's as though I was there only yesterday and the summer holidays had never happened. Nothing much has changed. I've been moved up into Form IV. Dishforth is the new Captain of Kitchener's. Frobisher is Captain of Jellicoe's. Briggs is Captain of Haig's and Head of School. Gore-Andrews is Captain of Trenchard's. Atwater is Captain of Rugger. Vole is Captain of Boxing.

Mr Bentham, Mr Warburton and Mr Wolf have all left. Someone called Miss Rump has taken over French from Mr Warburton. Mr Stapleford who was in the Royal Army Educational Corps is in charge of Carpentry, and someone called Mr Hill has taken over from Mr Wolf as our History master. He is much younger than Mr Wolf and has fair, curly hair and a huge moustache which sticks out on either side like the handlebars on Colin's bike. He was a Spitfire pilot in the war and won the DFC and Bar. He seems quite nice, not like a schoolmaster at all, and seems to know less about the Long Parliament than we do. Whenever he thinks we might be getting bored, he stops and tells us stories about the Battle of Britain.

When it got near Break, his right eye started twitching and as soon as the bell went, he ran out, jumped on his bike and cycled off up the road. Holmes-Johnson says that he probably got so used to running for his Spitfire during the Battle of Britain when the bell was rung at the dispersal hut and someone shouted 'Squadron scramble!' that now he rushes into action every time he hears a bell ringing.

Wetherby-Bell said, 'Perhaps he's gone up to Biggin Hill to get a Spitfire.' Colin said, 'Perhaps he'd gone to the Plumber's Arms to get a pint of beer.' Seabrook said, 'Perhaps he's just gone for a bike ride.' Holmes-Johnson said, 'Perhaps he's mad.' Colin said, 'You are, more likely,' and they had a terrific fight and Colin gave Holmes-Johnson a black eye and he had to go and see Matron.

If you ask me, I think the masters at our school are all completely batty.

Tuesday, September 25th

THIS afternoon we had rugger trials to see who would be playing in which Game. We all had to stand in a long line and when our name was called we had to try and tackle The Chimp. It took ages because he ran as fast as he could, holding a rugger ball, and got past before most boys could get anywhere near him, so they were made to try again until they did. He still managed to side-step most of them, or hand them off. Wetherby-Brown, who's one of the fastest runners in the school, got there before him and stood there waiting. The Chimp shouted, 'Come on, Brown. Don't stand there like a lump of lard. Get stuck in, boy.' Just as we thought he was going to do it, he turned round and ran off in the opposite direction with The Chimp running behind him. He finally caught up with him at the gate leading to Lower Field and brought him back by his ear. Wetherby-Brown said, 'Ow, sir, that really hurts.' The Chimp said, 'Not as much as it hurts me, Wetherby-Brown, and certainly not as much as it will hurt you when I give you six for gross cowardice.'

Atwater was the only one who managed to get his arms round his knees, but even when he did, The Chimp shouted, 'You still haven't got me down, Atwater,' and broke his tackle and ran on.

When it came to my turn, I pretended halfway across that I had sprained my ankle. I fell down and lay on the ground, holding it and groaning. The Chimp said, '*Typically* feeble, Bodge. Next!'

The only boy who managed to bring him down was Colin, who threw himself on the ground and stuck his hand out and tripped him. He came down with a terrific crash. When he got up he said, 'Not funny and not clever, Penwarden. Come and see me afterwards.'

He then said that he had never seen such an appalling display of moral slackness in his life and sent Forms III and IV off on a six-mile run. 'Perhaps that'll put a bit of backbone into you,' he said.

The run was supposed to be to Crockham Hill and back, but

Wetherby-Brown and Colin and I only went as far as Limpsfield Golf Course and hid in one of the huts until everyone came back and then we joined in and came back with them.

Even though it was a boiling day, we had compulsory hot drinks after Bath – hot Bovril or hot lemon squash. I hate both. At Julian's school they get given little green tins, about the size of Player's cigarette tins, with sweets in them – a barley sugar, a Horlicks tablet, a gum-drop, etc. Julian says they used to be given to the Army as emergency rations, but as the Army don't need them any more they give them to schools instead.

When I told Major Stanford-Dingley who was in charge with Matron, he said, 'We are not in an emergency situation.' I said that I was, because hot drinks made me feel sick and I was feeling really thirsty after the run.

He said, 'Thirsty? You don't know what thirst is, boy. Try crossing the Nefudh Desert with camels and only half a cup of water a day and you'll know what being thirsty is all about.'

Wednesday, September 26th

THE Games list went up today. I'm in Game III which is the lowest. At least I won't be picked for any matches, unlike Colin who's in Game I. But then he likes rugger. Perhaps it goes with being good at science.

Thursday, September 27th

WE had Mr Hill for History again. He was telling us about Charles I and his dealings with Cromwell when he suddenly stopped and asked us if we were bored. We all said yes, so he told us about the time his best friend was shot down in flames by an Me110. Luckily he landed in the English Channel just off Ramsgate, because the salt water was very good for his burns.

Pilbrow said his mother put soap on his finger when he picked up a hot saucepan and burned his finger.

Mr Hill said that he wasn't talking about fingers being burnt on saucepans, he was talking about people having their whole faces burnt off, and the skin on their legs hanging down like a pair of plus-fours, and their hands being so badly burnt that their fingers looked like birds' claws, and having to spend two or three years in hospital having bits of skin taken from different parts of their body which hadn't been burnt and grafted onto bits that had, so that they would have to spend the rest of their lives walking round looking like creatures from a freak show.

Seabrook asked what grafting meant and Mr Hill was about to explain when the bell for Break went and he rushed out of the room, jumped on his bike and rode off up the road.

Friday, September 28th

FISH for lunch. Today it was even more dried up and brown than usual, and tasted like smelly cardboard. Peskett asked Matron what it was and she said cod. Wetherby-Brown said, 'It must be the cod that passeth all understanding.' Matron sent him out of the room. Lucky him.

OCTOBER

Monday, October 1st

THIS morning the Major came to school in an armoured car. It has only a slit to look through, and a flap on the top of the turret instead of a proper door. When he got out he was wearing a leather jacket with a woolly lining and a leather helmet and goggles.

When Wetherby-Brown asked him if it was necessary to wear so much equipment, he said, 'If a thing's worth doing it's worth doing properly.'

Wetherby-Brown said, 'Did Lawrence of Arabia say that, sir?'

The Major said, 'No. Dr Johnson.'

I said, 'Is it true that Lawrence wore goggles when he was riding his camel in the desert?' He said, 'I'll give you goggles.'

I went to the school library and got out Boswell's *Life of Johnson* and looked right through it but I couldn't find the saying anywhere. It is only an abridged edition, but even so, it's got all the best bits in.

Friday, October 5th

I MENTIONED it to the Major at lunch today. He said, 'Are you doubting my word, you horrible little excrescence?' I said I had never doubted his word (I was crossing all my fingers and toes at the time), it was just that I wondered when exactly Dr Johnson had said this particular thing. He said, 'I don't know *exactly* when. Sitting on the lavatory, for all I know. I just happen to know he said it.' I said, 'With Boswell?' He asked me what I was babbling about. I said that Boswell wrote down everything Dr Johnson said and that if he had said this particular thing in the lavatory, Boswell would have had to be in there as well.

The Major started to go red in the face and said why should he have been? He wasn't a lavatory attendant. I said, in that case, how did he know he said it? The Major asked if I was trying to be funny. I said no. He asked me what I *was* trying to do. I said that the only reason we know what Dr Johnson said was because Boswell wrote it down, and if he didn't write this thing down, how do we know Dr Johnson said it?

The Major stared at me and pushed his moustache up with his forefinger. I thought for a moment he was going to tell me to go and stand outside The Chimp's study or something, but instead he said, 'It's a pity you don't put as much effort into your rugger as you do into trying to make me look an arse. Now shut up and get on with your tapioca.'

Dishforth said, 'Sir, did you know that Dr Johnson's cat was called Hodge?' The Major said, 'I don't like cats and I don't like people called Hodge.' And he got up, clipped me sharply round the ear and left the table.

Monday, October 8th

In Chapel this morning The Chimp said, 'We read in St Matthew that Jesus wept, but nowhere do we read that Jesus laughed. And yet I feel sure He must have had a good laugh with His Disciples from time to time. I bet all of them could tell a good joke when they wanted to and I bet Jesus told some of the best. Being the Son of God, if He couldn't make up a good joke, nobody could.'

When I told Daddy this, he said, 'This is the first time I've heard that Jesus and His Disciples were the Marx Brothers of their day.'

Tuesday, October 9th

Today the Major arrived with a trailer attached to the back of the armoured car, full of dustbins. When he left, it was empty.

Wednesday, October 10th

Today he came without the trailer.

Thursday, October 11th

SAME today. Mince for lunch. Wetherby-Brown said it reminded him of the time their cat got the squitters. None of us could eat anything after that. Mrs Harris came in and asked us if there was something wrong with the food. We told her we weren't feeling very hungry, but she said she wasn't going to see good food thrown away and that we'd have to sit there until we'd eaten everything that was on our plates.

We tried, but then Wetherby-Brown went 'miaow' and we all got the giggles and Holmes-Johnson did the nose trick and nearly choked. Matron got up and went across and banged him on the back and when that didn't work, she said, 'A warm douche for you, my lad,' and marched him off to Surgery. While she was away, we scraped half our mince onto Holmes-Johnson's plate and the rest onto hers. When she came back, we told her we hadn't cleared her plate because we knew she wouldn't want to see good food thrown away. She said, 'You haven't heard the end of this,' and she picked up her plate and walked out.

Friday, October 12th

TODAY the Major came with the trailer empty and when he left it was full of dustbins again. Wetherby-Brown thinks he may be smuggling something, but what? 'Masters who can't stand this place a moment longer?' said Holmes-Johnson.

Saturday, October 13th

AUNT Rowena has come to stay for the weekend. She is home on leave from India where she is the secretary to one of the governors out there. She lives in Government House and has lots of servants who do everything she wants. Mummy is very proud of her, even though she is much younger. She says she always was the cleverest of her family and always worked very hard, and that if I work hard I'll be able to have an interesting life like her.

We picked her up at the station. You could tell it was her as soon as she got off because she was easily the most glamorous person on the train. She looked a bit like Merle Oberon and even wore a little fur scarf kind of thing. When she got nearer you could see it was two foxes with their heads still on, biting each other's tails.

She smelt really whiffy when she kissed me. Nicer than Mummy, actually, but then, as Mrs Harrington said, 'You have to take what you can get on the scent counter of Boots these days.'

On the way home in the car I said, 'You're not very brown.' She said, '*You* are, but then I expect you've been out in the sun. The British in India never go out in the sun. If we did we'd finish up looking like the Indians, and that would be disastrous.' Mummy said that things weren't looking too clever for the British in India anyway, if the papers were anything to go by. Aunt Rowena said she didn't want to talk about it, so we didn't.

She didn't want to see our camp either, or play cricket. So she went to have a bath and relax before dinner. Mummy went up to see if she was all right and when she came down she said to Daddy, 'She's taken all the hot water. Her clothes are everywhere. She hasn't even emptied the bath. If she thinks I'm going to run round clearing up after her like one of her Indian servants, she's got another think coming.'

I wouldn't mind having servants to empty my bath and pick up my clothes when I grow up.

Sunday, October 14th

THE Urquarts and the Johnsons and Mrs Harrington and Mrs Pardoe came to drinks before lunch, but no girls, thank goodness. We had a tiny piece of pork for lunch.

Aunt Rowena said, 'You poor things, you really *are* having a hard time of it, aren't you?'

It rained after lunch so Daddy got out his old projector and showed some colour films that Aunt Rowena had brought back from India. There were lots of scenes of people walking around on lawns and having drinks and pulling faces at the camera and generally mucking about. She told us who they all were. One of them, a man in uniform with a big moustache, seemed to be in every shot, standing next to her, talking and grinning. She said his name was Geoffrey and he was one of the Governor's ADCs. Mummy said, 'Is he sweet on you?' Aunt Rowena said, 'Of course not, he's just a friend.' Mummy said, 'He looks as if he's sweet on you.' She said, 'Well, he isn't, so there.'

The other reel was of some festival in the nearby town. There were lots of scenes with elephants wearing bright costumes and jewellery, and men in loincloths playing drums and leaping about and doing dangerous things with flaming torches. There were also lots more shots of English people pulling silly faces, and of Geoffrey trying to grab hold of Aunt Rowena and her laughing and trying to push him away.

'He looks pretty sweet on you, if you ask me,' said Mummy. If you ask me, too, but nobody did.

I wouldn't at all mind living in India when I grow up.

Monday, October 15th

ACCORDING to Wetherby-Brown, Mr Hill *does* go to the Plumber's Arms every Break, and every lunchtime, and every evening, too. He found out by going down there and asking the landlord. Apparently he said we were doing a report for our Geography master on the distribution and usages of hops in the south of England. If what the landlord says is true, it might explain why Mr Hill is so hazy about the reign of Charles I.

It's probably not the only thing he's hazy about. I read a thing in the *Sunday Express* once about the effect that war can have on people's behaviour, and a lot of people who've been in battles find that the only way they can get over it afterwards is by drinking a lot. I'm wondering if that's what's happened to Mr Hill. If so, I'm really sorry because I really like him.

I hope Daddy's not suffering from the effects of being a Desert Rat. He's always going to the pub with Dickie Pargeter. On the other hand, Mummy still drinks quite a lot of gin and she hasn't been in any battles, except ones with Daddy in the kitchen in the evenings.

Tuesday, October 16th

MAJOR Stanford-Dingley brought the dustbins again today and left without them. He must be up to something. We obviously can't ask him straight out what. Wetherby-Brown,

who listens in to all the programmes on 'Children's Hour' about Norman and Henry Bones, the boy detectives, has come up with a plan and if the Major does the same as last week we're going to try it out on Friday afternoon.

Wednesday, October 17th

N o trailer today.

Thursday, October 18th

S AME as yesterday.
I got home this evening to find that the chrysalis was empty and there was a butterfly on the twig next to it. It's quite nice – sort of brown with black spots – but not as nice as I had hoped. After tea I took the lid off the jar and it flew off down the garden. Mummy said, 'It'll probably get eaten by a bird after all.' I said, 'Yes, but at least it will have had a more interesting life than it would have done as just a caterpillar.'

I probably won't bother to tell Julian.

Friday, October 19th

T HE Major arrived with an empty trailer, just like last week, and after school he and Murch, the school odd-job man, started to load up. Dishforth kept *cave* while we got the rocks and big stones which we'd collected and hidden in the rhododendrons beside the school gates and put them all over the drive. When Dishforth gave the signal that he was about to leave, we ran across the road onto the Common and hid in the bracken. The Major came roaring out of the drive. We thought he would drive over the rocks and that the dustbins would tip over so we'd be able to see what was inside, or who,

but instead, when the front wheel went over the first rock the armoured car bounced about four feet in the air, there was a loud bang inside and it stopped.

For a moment nothing happened and then the turret flew open and the Major's head popped out. He pulled off his helmet and we could see this whacking great red bump on the top of his bald head. You could actually see it getting bigger all the time. He shouted 'Right!', then he dived down into the turret and a few moments later came up with a pair of binoculars and looked through them. At one point he looked straight at the place where we were hiding and we thought he must have seen us, but in the end he hung the binoculars round his neck and said 'Right!' again very loudly and disappeared back inside the turret. Then he revved up the engine and drove very slowly out of the drive and away down the road towards Hurst Green.

Monday, October 22nd

WHEN the Major came into Chapel this morning, he still had quite a large bump on his head. Wetherby-Brown whispered, 'When he leaves he could always get a job as a Belisha beacon.' We all got the giggles and I had to push my handkerchief in my mouth.

The Chimp gave a talk about Jesus, the Great Cavalry Commander, and then said, 'Many brave soldiers have tried to follow Our Lord onto the enemy guns; few have succeeded like the man we are proud to number amongst the staff of this school. An officer whose name is synonymous with armoured warfare. A hero not of this latest conflict, but of an earlier one, whom Lawrence of Arabia, no less, was proud to number amongst his friends, and at whose shoulder he rode and helped to drive the infidel Turk from Palestine.

'I speak, of course, of Major Stanford-Dingley. A kind, gentle and brave man who has nothing but the good of this school at heart. And yet on Friday afternoon, while driving out through the school gates, taking with him the potato peelings and apple cores and unwanted leftovers that are so carelessly left by you boys and are so necessary for the pigs that he rears on his small-holding, some of you saw fit to subject him to a vicious and cowardly attack, the results of which are plain to see.'

The Chimp then said that he expected those responsible to see him in his study immediately afterwards. If no one had the guts to own up, the whole school would be severely punished.

In a Biggles book I read once, it said that the blood drained from Ginger's face. I now know what it means. In fact, Wetherby-Brown's face had turned almost the same colour as his grey school shirt.

We met afterwards in the changing room to decide on our plan of campaign. Holmes-Johnson said he knew exactly what we should do and when we said 'What?' he said, 'Run away and join the French Foreign Legion.'

At that moment Briggs came in and said, 'I hope you lot are not thinking of doing anything silly.' We said we didn't know what he was talking about. Briggs said, 'You know very well what I'm talking about. Gore-Andrews saw what you did and told me. I could have reported you to the Head Man, but I didn't. I may be Head Boy but I'm not a sneak.'

Wetherby-Brown said, 'It was only meant as a joke, Briggs.' Briggs said, 'So what? All I know is that if you don't own up we're all going to be in the soup.' Holmes-Johnson said, 'Keep your hair on, Briggs. Of course we're going to own up. What did you think we were going to do?'

When we went to see The Chimp he said, 'I won't mince words. This is a beating matter. I am impressed by the fact that you all owned up at once. On the other hand, I feel that as senior boys you should be setting an example to the younger ones and that I would be failing in my duty if I were to let you off scot-free. I shall sleep on the matter and deliver my verdict in the morning.'

I am writing this in the camp. I haven't told Mummy and Daddy about what happened yet. The trouble is, the Army edition of 'Merry-Go-Round' is on the wireless tonight, with Cheerful Charlie Chester and His Crazy Gang, and I really like listening in to that with Mummy and Daddy. Not that I really understand all the jokes, but I like the way Daddy laughs and it makes me laugh too, and I wouldn't want to spoil it by telling them I'm in trouble. I might tell them afterwards.

I DIDN'T in the end. We had such a nice evening and everyone laughed so much that I just couldn't. I also couldn't get to sleep for hours and when I did, I kept having horrible dreams about being in a tent in the desert with Major Stanford-Dingley and him being dressed as an Arab sheikh and beating me with a huge hairy caterpillar, and then waking up, which I did about a hundred million times.

I couldn't eat any breakfast and kept wanting to go to the lavatory. Mummy asked if I was feeling all right. I very nearly said no and could she ring up and say I was ill, but I didn't want to let the others down, so I said I was fine.

The first thing I saw when I got to school was a stream of boys going across the 1st XV rugger pitch from the Headmaster's house to the school. A few were limping, some were hopping up and down holding their bottoms, some had their arms round each other, one or two were crying. It reminded me of a picture in a book I've got about the First World War, called *The Retreat from Mons*.

At first I thought The Chimp must have slept on it and decided to set an example and punish the whole school, and the blood ran from my face again. But when I asked Dishforth, he said a packet of Player's Weights had been found in Blenheim dorm and no one would own up, so the whole dormitory had been beaten, plus Ramillies, Oudenarde and Malplaquet.

The Chimp sent for us after Chapel. He said, 'I have thought long and hard about this matter and I have talked with Major Stanford-Dingley. It has not escaped our notice that all your fathers, with the sad exception of Mr Holmes-Johnson, have served with distinction in various theatres of war, and Major Stanford-Dingley agrees with me that to ask the sons of fellow officers to bend over while the sounds of battle are still fresh in their fathers' ears would be too much to expect. I have therefore decided to fit the punishment to the crime in this case, and so instead of games this afternoon, you will all run down to Major Stanford-Dingley's smallholding where you will muck out his pigs and then run back again.'

He asked us if we had anything to say. Holmes-Johnson asked if we could all be beaten instead. The Chimp said,

'Given that your father wriggled out of military service on the feeble pretext of flat feet, Holmes-Johnson, I would suggest that you are pushing your luck.'

In the end it wasn't as bad as all that, actually. Wetherby-Brown grumbled about missing rugger, but as far as I was concerned, mucking out pigs was like a day at the seaside compared with Game III.

When I got home, Mummy asked if I was feeling better. I said I was, much. She asked me what I'd been doing and I told her we ran to Major Stanford-Dingley's and back. She said it sounded to her like a case of kill or cure. Then she said I'd better have a bath. Where had I been? Rolling in a pigsty? I just laughed.

It was pork brawn and salad for supper, but I just had some home-made tomato soup and a piece of mousetrap and went to bed early with an apple and a book called *David Goes to Zululand*. It's about a fourteen-year-old boy who gets sent to Africa and makes friends with a black boy called Obit and they are taught to hunt big game by a famous Zulu hunter. It isn't bad if you like that sort of thing.

I feel really sorry for Holmes-Johnson. It must be awful to know you're the only one whose father wasn't in the war.

Wednesday, October 24th

TODAY in Chapel Chimp Harris announced that the House Boxing Competition will take place a week today. The film afterwards will be *San Demetrio, London*. When I asked Major Stanford-Dingley, who's in charge of boxing this term, why we can't have the film on another day, he said, 'Pleasure can only be fully enjoyed after pain – as you will discover for yourself a week today.'

Thursday, October 25th

MR Hill didn't turn up for Double History this afternoon and The Chimp had to come and teach us instead. He said, 'There are only two things you have to understand about Charles I. One is that he was a Roman Catholic and the other is that he was less than five foot tall. Understand those two things and the whole story of the English Civil War falls into place.'

Friday, October 26th

Why am I always picked to box people who are much bigger than me? This time it's Gilbert. Not only is he about twice my size, but it is well known that he is the worst bully in the school. His mother told Colin's mother who told Mummy who told me that when he first arrived at Badger's Mount as a boarder aged ten and a half, she asked him if there was any bullying. He said there was, lots. She said, 'How awful. Who's responsible?' Gilbert said proudly, 'Oh, I am.'

When Mummy raised the subject of bullying with The Chimp, he said, 'In my experience, it's good for a boy's character to be faced with unequal odds. Horatius was faced with unequal odds when he came up against Lars Porsena of Clusium, and it certainly brought out the best in *him*.'

Sunday, October 28th

According to the wireless, an RAF jet has flown at 540 mph. Colin's worked out that's 12 yards a second! He said that one day a jet will be able to fly at the speed of sound, which is 720 mph. I know he's quite good at science, but honestly!

Tuesday, October 30th

I woke up really early, about five, and lay there wondering what it would feel like to be smashed in the face by Gilbert. I once got into a fight with Peskett but that was only because I happen to know his father's a vicar, also because he can't see very well without his glasses, also because he's even worse at rugger tackling than I am. Even so, he hit me on the nose and it jolly well hurt. My eyes watered and my nose bled like billy-o and I had to lie down on the changing-room floor and have a cold key put down my back.

Gilbert's twice as big as Peskett, and he's in the 1st XV

97

scrum, and he doesn't wear glasses, and his father runs a lorry firm in Redhill. Obviously I have to go to ordinary boxing every Wednesday like everyone else, but I'm no good and never get asked to spar with the Major like Holmes-Johnson and Vole and the other good people. Gilbert always spars with the Major, and he does extra boxing after school on Friday afternoons. I don't stand an earthly.

Then I had a brainwave. I got up early and wrote a letter to Major Stanford-Dingley saying how sorry I was about what we'd done and I hoped his head was getting better. I left it in his pigeon-hole as soon as I got to school. It was still there in Break and at Lunch and after Hot Drinks. When I asked The Chimp's secretary, Miss Balls, why, she said, 'I have no idea. I am not my brother's keeper, or Major Stanford-Dingley's. I daresay he'll collect it before he goes home.'

Just William was on 'Children's Hour' for the first time ever. A boy called John Clark plays William. He's really good and really funny. Actually, I always think Wetherby-Brown and Dishforth and I are a bit like the Outlaws. Today's story was about William running away and pretending to be the new boots boy in a big house and being bossed about by the butler and shoving a blacking brush in his face. I've always wanted to be William, but never as much as I do now it's the Boxing Competition.

Wednesday, October 31st

THE worst day of term. I couldn't eat any breakfast again and when Mummy asked why, I said I had a headache and could I be off school for the day? She took my temperature and although I rubbed my tongue on the end as hard as I could while she wasn't looking, it was still normal. She said, 'You'll cry wolf once too often,' and said if I didn't look sharp I'd be late for Chapel. I told her that actually I was thinking of becoming a Hindu. 'Not today, you're not,' she said.

As soon as I got to school I went to look at the masters' pigeon-holes and the Major's was empty. I passed him in the

corridor after Chapel but he didn't say anything about it. I saw him again in Break and asked him if he'd got my letter. 'Yes, thank you,' he said. I said I was really sorry and that I'd got a bit of a headache and would it be all right if Holmes-Johnson boxed Gilbert and I boxed Wentworth? He said, 'If you think I haven't got better things to do than start rewriting the timetable, you've got another think coming,' and he walked off into the staff room.

I was standing outside the changing room after lunch when Mrs Harris came past and said, 'What's the matter with you? You look like a wet weekend in Brighton.' I explained about having to box Gilbert and how he's the school bully and everything. She said, 'In my experience there's only one way to deal with bullies. A good hard punch on the nose.'

The boxing competition started at 2.30. We don't have a proper ring or anything, just a few tables put round in a square. Everyone in the school has to take part, starting with the new boys and working up to Form IV, so it takes absolutely ages. By the time it came to the Form IIs, the whole floor was covered with blood and so were the boxing-gloves. Everyone was shouting and screaming so loud you couldn't hear it when anyone got hurt. While I was waiting to go in, I said to Gilbert, 'I won't hit you hard if you don't hit me hard.' Gilbert said, 'You couldn't hit me hard if you tried.' I told him I'd give him all my sweets for the rest of term. He said, 'Everyone says that. I've got more sweets than I can eat.' I said, 'How about doing all your Latin preps for you for the rest of term?' He said, 'For the rest of the year?' I said, 'Okay.' He said, 'Okay, then.'

I saw Mrs Harris there while I was having my gloves tied on and I smiled at her, but she didn't smile back.

When we touched gloves the Major said, 'Right, boys. A good clean fight, now. No punching below the belt or on the back of the neck, and no kicking or biting.'

I thought we'd just shuffle about a bit and pretend to hit each but actually hit each other's gloves, but when the bell went, Gilbert came straight up to me and before I'd even had a chance to put my gloves up, he hit me really hard right in the eye.

At first I couldn't see anything at all, and he hit me lots more times. But then I turned my back on him and he couldn't. The Major got hold of me by the shoulder and said, 'Stop arsing about and box on.' Gilbert was standing on the other side of him, grinning like an ape.

I got really angry then, and before the Major had time to step aside I ran forward and hit Gilbert as hard as I could, right on the nose. Blood shot out all over the floor. Gilbert yelled 'Ouch!' and put his hands up to feel his face, so I hit him really hard in the solar plexus and he fell onto the floor and lay there, doubled-up, while the Major counted to ten and called out, 'Blue's the winner.' Gilbert couldn't breathe properly for ages. I was really quite worried. I was even more worried when he was helped past me by Matron and taken up to Surgery. He said, 'Just you wait.'

In the end Kitchener's beat Haig's easily, Jellicoe's came third and Trenchard's came fourth. Mrs Harris presented the House Boxing Cup after tea to Dishforth and then we all had to go up and shake her hand. She had put on an extra layer of make-up for the occasion. When it came to my turn she said, 'Congratulations.' I said, 'I did what you told me.' She said, 'What did I tell you?' I said about punching Gilbert on the nose. She said, 'I can't imagine why I should have said that. I know absolutely nothing about boxing.' As well as smelling of powder, she smelt like Mummy does sometimes when she's had a few gins.

In the evening we had the film of *San Demetrio, London*. It's all about this tanker in the war called *San Demetrio* that catches on fire and the crew have to abandon ship and then they drift around for a few days but decide they'd be better off on board, so they find the ship again and get back on board and put the fires out and sail it back to Scotland and get given a huge amount of money for salvaging it. It was quite exciting in places, but I didn't enjoy it much because my eye hurt every time I blinked.

Also, I was sitting next to the man who worked the projector and he kept talking to me all the time and saying things like 'There's a good bit coming', 'You'll like this bit', etc. Once when some of the men were climbing down the side of the ship, he leaned forward and said, 'It's all faked, of course. If you tip your head sideways, you can see they're actually crawling along the floor on their hands and knees.' Thanks to him, I may never enjoy a film again.

NOVEMBER

Thursday, November 1st

WHEN I came down to breakfast this morning, Daddy said, 'That's a real shiner you've got there. How did you come by that?' When I told him, the boxing competition, he said, 'Did you win?' I said yes. He said, 'Good man!' and gave my shoulder a little squeeze.

Gilbert wasn't in class today. Good.

Friday, November 2nd

HALF-TERM began at lunchtime. A lot of the boarders went off to catch the school train, including Gilbert. He said to me, 'We'll sort this business out once and for all when we come back. Without gloves.'

According to the *Daily Express*, there have been rumours that Hitler isn't dead at all and that he escaped from Berlin and is hiding somewhere, but now they know he definitely is. Dead, I mean. I wish Gilbert was.

Saturday, November 3rd

THIS morning I went with Daddy in the car down to Oxted to do the shopping and he bought me a liquorice shoelace. We met Dickie Pargeter who said why didn't we pop up to Tankards and have a glass of something. It was pretty boring. Daddy and Dickie Pargeter looked round the garden for ages, and I was made to play with Timothy who's only nine and his sister Elizabeth who's four and tried to bite my leg. Mrs Pargeter, whose name is Olive, asked me if I'd like a Tizer and

I said yes, please. So she went to get some, but when she came back, she said they'd run out and would I like a lemon squash instead and I said no, thank you.

After ages Daddy and Dickie Pargeter came back in and had gin-and-limes with Mrs Pargeter. Daddy had two and Mr and Mrs Partridge had three. Dickie was wearing the worst clothes I've ever seen. There were holes in the elbows of his sports jacket, his knees were sticking through his trousers and his shoes were falling to bits. His hair was what Mummy would have called 'all over his head'. He looked as I imagine Worzel Gummidge would look like in real life.

When Dickie asked how I was getting on at school, Daddy said, 'Guy's showing promise as a boxer.' Dickie said, 'Good lad,' and tried to box me. I boxed him back and hit him by mistake really hard in his thing and he had to go and lie down. Daddy said, 'I hope they don't teach you to box like that at school.'

Sunday, November 4th

I was going across the Common on my bike this morning when a gang of village boys suddenly appeared in the middle of the path and blocked it. I tried to cycle past, but couldn't. One of them who was absolutely huge, even bigger than The Chimp, snatched my RAF cap off my head. I told him to give it back. He said, 'Why should I?' and threw it to one of the others. I tried to catch it, but then they all started throwing it to each other and I couldn't.

Then the huge one got it. I said, 'Please give it back.' Then they all started imitating me and saying 'Please, please,' and laughing and throwing the cap around again. I tried to get back on my bike, but the huge one stood right in front of me and held on to my handlebars and said, 'Where do you think you're going?' I said I had to get home for lunch. He said, 'Sorry, we haven't finished with you yet,' and he threw the cap to one of the others again.

I said, 'If you don't give me back my cap . . .' He said, 'You'll what?' and pushed his face very close to mine and gurked really loudly, right in my face. Then everyone laughed and made gurking noises, so I kicked him as hard as I could on the shin. Luckily I was wearing my black leather shoes. He went bright red in the face and leaned forward and I punched him on the nose. I think I might have broken it because it made a horrible cracking sound and blood flew out everywhere. He yelled with pain and put his hands up to his face, so I kicked him on his other shin and he fell on the ground and lay there moaning. The others just stood there staring. I said, 'May I have my cap back, please?' The one who was holding it threw it to me, and then they all ran away and I got on my bike and rode home.

When I told Daddy what had happened, he said, 'Well done, tadpole. It's a pity someone didn't do that to Hitler in 1938.'

Monday, November 5th

THE end of half-term. Mr Hill has left. The Headmaster announced it in Chapel. He said it was for personal reasons and that the school had lost not only a highly valued member of staff but a war hero whose guts and patriotism were an inspiration to us all. Dishforth whispered, 'Not to me.'

Afterwards I overheard Stuffy Bedding saying to Gnasher Davies, 'I wouldn't give a lot for Hill's guts with the quantity of beer he's downed in the last few weeks.'

Someone called Mr Horsburgh is our new History master. He's a retired Air Marshal, so everyone was wondering what to call him. When Wetherby-Brown asked him, he said, 'Air Marshal will do.'

While we were having half-term, Murch built the biggest bonfire I've ever seen. After school we all had to sit in our classrooms for ages. In the end someone rang the school bell and we all went down to Lower Field. The Chimp asked if anyone had brought their own fireworks. One or two boys put their hands up, including Wetherby-Brown and Dishforth. He said, 'No one is allowed to set off any fireworks without per-mission from me.'

We were then made to stand in a huge circle round the fire while The Chimp and Murch and some of the other masters tried to light it. The wood must have been damp or something, because although the newspaper burnt well, nothing else did and it kept fizzling out. In the end Murch had to throw some petrol on it and very nearly set *himself* on fire.

The Guy looked like Dickie Pargeter, only better dressed.

Gilbert and his friends were standing nearby. I thought he was going to make one of his feeble jokes about me being called Guy, like he always does, but he pretended he hadn't seen me and walked off in the opposite direction. I think that deep down he's really wet.

Once the fire had got under way, Matron and Mrs Harris put some potatoes in the hot ashes to cook. Then Major Stanford-Dingley and the Air Marshal set off some fireworks. They were hopeless. The Catherine Wheel was especially feeble. It went round very slowly once and then fell off, but then Catherine Wheels always do. The Golden Rain was okay. There were only two rockets. The first one went onto the school roof and Murch had to run all the way up the hill to see if the school was on fire, which it wasn't, worse luck. The second one was just about to go off when the milk bottle it was in fell over and it shot straight into the crowd and hit Gilbert in the eye and he had to go to hospital. Now he's got a black eye too. Everyone got terribly worried, but I couldn't have cared less.

In the excitement Matron forgot all about the baked potatoes, and when she remembered she found they had all burnt to a frazzle, but we were made to eat them anyway. Mrs Harris said, 'Waste not, want not.' I definitely didn't want mine and neither did anyone else, so we all threw them into the bushes when no one was looking.

Then The Chimp called out that if anyone wanted to let off their fireworks, would they report to him. Wetherby-Brown and one or two others went forward. They were all sent off to a corner of Lower Field and told to stand well clear when they'd lit the blue touch paper, and not to point anything at anyone.

We all stood there waiting, staring into the dark but not able to see a thing. Then we saw a match being lit and then I don't know what happened except that there were fireworks going off in every direction and bangers and rockets whizzing over our heads and everything. The Chimp shouted out, 'Everyone lie flat on the ground and don't move till I tell you.' The ground was completely soaking, but we thought we'd better do what we were told and we all got covered in mud. The Major, who was standing nearby, said, 'If you think this is bad, you should have been with Lawrence when we attacked the Turks in the night at Akaba.'

Then suddenly it all stopped and Wetherby-Brown's voice called out, 'Sorry, sir. Bit of a bish.'

The Chimp said, 'I'll give you a bish, Brown. Outside my study. Tomorrow morning. Eight o'clock.'

Suddenly it began to pour with rain and the fire started to go out and we all had to go in.

Wednesday, November 7th

A GLOSTER Meteor jet has just flown over Herne Bay in Kent at 606 mph. That's ten miles a minute! It's incredible! Perhaps Colin was right after all, and an aeroplane *can* go at the speed of sound.

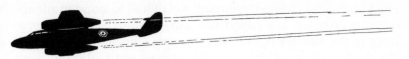

Sunday, November 11th

TODAY was Remembrance Day. There was a special service at the school and we all had to stand round the memorial to the boys and masters who were killed in the Great War and sing special hymns. One went 'Oh valiant hearts something something something' and was really sad. I couldn't help thinking about Uncle Tony who was killed in the Battle of Arnhem and I very nearly cried.

Bostridge actually did cry, but then his father was killed in a bomber over Germany. I felt really sorry for him. It must be awful not having a father. I didn't have one for a while but I knew that I did really and could look forward to him coming home. When he first did, I wasn't quite as glad as I thought I would be. I knew he was my father, but it didn't feel as though he was, sort of thing. It's difficult to explain. Anyway, it was very queer. Actually, I don't think he really knew who I was, either. I mean, he knew I was his son, but it didn't seem like that. He didn't give me any hugs or anything. He still doesn't, but I don't really mind. I'd rather have a father who doesn't hug me than not have one at all. Compared with Bostridge and my cousins, I'm really lucky.

Besides, Daddy and I are having much more fun together than we did. The other day we were in Limpsfield High Street and he suddenly said, 'God, this is a dull place. Let's ring all the front doorbells and run away.'

We stood in the doorway of the book shop and watched all the people up and down the street opening their doors and looking up and down at each other and going back in again. One of them, an old woman, shouted out, 'Bloody kids, just let me get my hands on them.' I've never seen a grown-up laugh as much as Daddy did. I thought he was going to explode. He said, 'Don't you dare tell Mummy, or we'll both be in Queer Street.' I wasn't going to.

Anyway, after we'd sung the hymns, The Chimp read out something about the people who had died never growing old like the rest of us and Bostridge cried again. Then the school clock started to chime eleven and we all had to stand in silence for two minutes. It's called the Two-Minute Silence. Everybody in the country does it. Even people who are driving along the road in their cars have to stop and get out and stand there without moving or saying anything for two minutes. You don't realise how long two minutes is unless you've stood still for that long without moving or speaking.

When it was over, the music master, Mr Trimble, stepped forward and played The Last Post on a trumpet. He kept bishing up the notes and once he made a noise that was exactly like someone letting off. I had to bite the inside of my mouth to stop myself laughing, and made it bleed. Then the House Captains walked forward with wreaths made of paper poppies and stood there in front of everyone. Dishforth gave his to Mr Horsburgh who went and laid it on the memorial on behalf of the Air Force. Frobisher gave his to Major Stanford-Dingley who did the same thing on behalf of the Army, and Gore-Andrews gave his to the Headmaster. I didn't know The Chimp had been in the Navy.

Briggs laid one on behalf of the school. Everyone bowed, then we sang 'God Save the King' and then we all went home. At least, Colin and I did. We sang silly songs all the way. We were half-way across the Common when we saw the village boys coming along the path towards us. The huge one had a plaster across his nose and both his eyes were black-and-blue.

Colin said, 'Let's go the other way.' I said, 'Keep going. They won't do anything to us.' Colin said, 'How do you know?' I said, 'I bet they won't.' He said, 'How much?' I said, 'Threepence.' He said, 'Okay.' We were about twenty yards away when the village boys suddenly stopped and stood there. Colin said, 'You owe me threepence.' At that moment the huge boy pointed to a path nearby and they all walked off up it. I said to Colin, 'You owe *me* threepence.'

When we were quite a long way away, Colin asked how I knew they weren't going to do anything. I said I didn't, it was just a guess. He obviously didn't believe me so I told him what happened on Sunday. He said, 'I didn't know you were any good at fighting.' I said, 'I'm not, but *they* think I am and that's all that matters.' Colin said, 'Oh, right,' but I don't think he really understood.

Just William has been moved from 'Children's Hour' to 8.45 in the evening. Have the BBC gone mad?

Monday, November 12th

WHEN I woke up this morning I had such a bad sore throat I could hardly swallow. It felt as if I had a whole lot of ping-pong balls in my throat. When I told Mummy she said, 'Cod-liver oil for you.' I wish I hadn't said anything now. I really hate cod-liver oil. It's the worst taste in the world, even worse than hot Bovril.

I asked Mummy why the bottle has a fisherman on it with a huge cod hanging over his shoulder, smiling in a nice friendly way as if you're really going to like it, when nobody does. (I meant, the fisherman's smiling, not the cod.) She said that if it had a horrible fisherman on it and he was scowling and looking really unfriendly, no one would buy the stuff. That's what advertising's all about, making things that aren't very nice look nicer than they really are. I said, did that mean it isn't true that Palmolive gives you a schoolgirl complexion? Mummy said she was sure it would if you happened to be a schoolgirl. I said, what about the nice old shoemender with the glasses on the end of his nose who says, 'Take it from me . . . Phillips Rubber Soles and Heels double the life of your shoes!' Was he telling the truth? Mummy said she was sure that if you stuck rubber soles and heels on your new shoes they'd last longer than if you didn't, but she doubted if they would make them last *twice* as long.

I said, so was advertising just another word for lying? She said, not really, it was more a question of trying to persuade people something's better than it really is.

This has come as quite a surprise to me. I always thought that everything people wrote in the newspapers was true. When Daddy came down to breakfast I said, 'You know that advertisement for Erasmic that says, "Not too little . . . not too much . . . but just right, thanks to the double dense lather of Erasmic shaving stick"? You always use Erasmic. Is it true? Does it really have double dense lather?' Daddy said, 'I've no idea.' I said, 'Why do you buy it, then?' He said, 'It's the only one they stock in Douthwaite's.'

All I know is that I wish I could have Radio Malt instead of cod-liver oil. Colin let me try some of his once. It's really delicious, a bit like Tate and Lyle's Golden Syrup but with much more taste. He always has it, and he never gets a cold. I told Mummy, but all she said was, 'I'll see.' That usually means no.

Friday, November 16th

An amazing thing happened today. We were all mucking about outside during Break when a small aeroplane flew low over the woods and the pilot leant out of the cockpit and started bombing the roof of the school with bags of flour. Everyone cheered like mad until the front door opened and The Chimp came running out with the rest of the staff and made us all take cover indoors. The pilot went on bombing the school for ages. Wetherby-Brown and I were watching from the Form IV window when the plane came down so low it almost hit one of the chimneys. As the pilot banked away he suddenly pulled his helmet and goggles off and waved and we realised it was Mr Hill. We all waved back and cheered and he wiggled his wings in a Victory wave and flew off in the direction of Westerham.

We were all told to go into the Dining Room and wait. After a while The Chimp came in and said, 'You may think what you have just witnessed was an amusing example of youthful high spirits, but I'm afraid you are sadly mistaken. Mr Hill is a brave man. No doubt about it. He is one of The Few. If it had not been for the likes of him we would long since have been ground beneath the heel of the jackboot. However, there is a price to be paid for everything in this world, and in Mr Hill's case that price was his sanity. The man who came here at the beginning of this term to teach History to Forms III and IV was an empty husk, sustained only by drink and memories. I would dearly have loved to keep him on, but it was not to be. It was my understanding that he was equally anxious to move on, but I see now that I was wrong and he has made his feelings known in no uncertain terms – as, I have no doubt, will the Powers-that-Be. In the meantime, I would ask you all to put this unhappy incident out of your minds and pray that Mr Hill will find the peace of mind he so clearly longs for and so richly deserves. And will the boy who attempted to flush Bostridge's plimsolls down the first-floor lavatory kindly report to me in the study immediately after morning school?'

Saturday, November 17th

I CAME down this morning to find Daddy had got his stamp album out. We sat down together and went through it. He said he began collecting when he was about my age, but had stopped when war broke out.

A lot of his stamps are from countries I've never heard of before, like Antioquia and Condinamarca and Stellaland, which is now part of Bechuanaland, and the Oils River Protectorate which has Queen Victoria's head on it and is now Nigeria, and Van Diemen's Land which is now Tasmania. He's got some Cape Triangulars which he says are quite rare, and several from somewhere called Fernando Po, which is an island in Spanish Guinea I've never heard of.

He's also got quite a big collection commemorating the Coronation of the King and Queen from places like the British Solomon Islands and the

Somaliland Protectorate and the Gold Coast. Also a lot of American stamps with the heads of the Presidents on them, and several pages of old English stamps, including a Penny Red. I was really excited and said that Peskett, who has the biggest collection in the school, told me that Penny Reds were very valuable.

Daddy said he must have meant the Penny Black and that sadly he didn't have one. Still, a Penny Red is pretty good.

I said, why didn't I start collecting stamps? I could specialise in the British Empire and he could do Europe and the Rest of the World or something. He said, 'Good idea. I'll think about it.'

Monday, November 19th

IN Chapel this morning The Chimp said that no one had owned up about Bostridge's plimsolls. He said, 'We didn't spend the last six years defeating Nazism in order that people should take other people's plimsolls whenever they feel like it and flush them down lavatories and not own up afterwards. The Romans had a saying, *Nemo me impune lacessit*. Anyone?'

Seabrook put his hand up and said, 'Only the puny put plimsolls down the lavatory, sir?' and everyone laughed.

The Chimp said, 'Typically idiotic, Seabrook. In fact it means "No one provokes me unpunished", as you will discover for yourself in my study afterwards.'

He then said he was going to count up to ten and if no one owned up then he would have no alternative but to punish the entire school. No one did, so we've all got to run round Lower Field twenty times after school tomorrow.

On the way out, Briggs said to Seabrook that since he was going to be beaten anyway, why didn't he say *he'd* done it. Seabrook said, 'But I didn't.' Briggs said, 'So what?' Seabrook said, 'I don't see why I should if I didn't.' Briggs said, 'God, you're a drip. I bet your father wasn't in the war.' Seabrook said, 'That just shows how much you know.' Briggs said, 'What regiment?' Seabrook said, 'He was in the Navy, actually.' Briggs said, 'Oh really? Which ship?' Seabrook said, 'He went down with HMS *Hood*.' Briggs went red in the face and said, 'Gosh, I'm really sorry, Seabrook, I didn't realise,' and walked off in a hurry.

Wetherby-Brown said, 'Was your father really on the *Hood*,

Brooky?' Seabrook said, 'Don't be silly. How could he have been? He got three wickets in the Fathers' Match last term.'

Monday, November 26th

YESTERDAY Daddy got his lead soldiers out. They weren't quite as good as he remembered. An awful lot of them had bits missing – legs, arms, swords, plumes, bayonets, whole heads sometimes. They were in an even worse state than my farm animals. Unfortunately, the British were more badly damaged than the foreigners. There was a whole platoon of Venezuelan Cavalry that looked as though they had never seen any action, and the Capetown Highlanders were only missing one leg between them. But every one of the eleven 21st Lancers was missing an arm or a leg or something, and only the bugler had escaped without a wound.

We were able to stick some of the heads back on using matchsticks, and Daddy managed to solder on one or two of the horses' legs using his Fluxite Soldering Set. We tried to attach the bayonets but it was no use, and in the end we had to leave them lying in the bottom of the box.

Daddy said, 'In war the winners always seem to come off worse than the losers,' and he got really down in the dumps and put them all away again.

Tuesday, November 27th

WE had dead leg and cabbage for lunch today. I had to hold my nose all the time, but even so I could still taste it. I didn't really agree with Daddy on Sunday about winners and losers, but I do now.

DECEMBER

Saturday, December 8th

DADDY and I were in Oxted doing the shopping this morning when he suddenly said, 'There's Peter Harrington!' and pointed to the other side of the road. I can't remember exactly what Julian's father looks like, but there's a photograph of him on a table in their drawing room in mess kit with fair curly hair and a moustache and a nice smiling face, and the man coming out of the ironmonger's didn't look anything like that. I said, 'Are you sure?' and he said, 'Well, it looks like him.' I said, 'But I thought Julian's father was the same age as you. That man looks really old and thin and he's walking with a stick and he's hardly got any hair.' Daddy said he must have made a mistake.

When we got home we told Mummy we thought we'd seen him, but it couldn't have been. She said it was him. She'd seen Julian in the road. He's on exeat for the weekend. The reason they hadn't had any news for so long wasn't because he was stuck in the jungle, but in a Jap prisoner-of-war camp. According to Julian, he'd been in there for months. She said, 'We all thought the Germans treated their POWs badly but it was nothing compared with the things the Japs did.' When I asked her what sort of things, she said she didn't want to go into details, but apparently Mrs Harrington hadn't recognised him when he got off the train at the station. I asked why he had a stick. Mummy said, 'I didn't ask.'

I remember being with Julian and seeing some photographs in a window in Oxted some time during the summer holidays of people who had been prisoners in German concentration camps. Some of them were so thin they looked like skeletons with bits of skin stretched over them. It's the only time I can remember when Julian hasn't known what to say.

Sunday, December 9th

I was on my bike going down to see Colin this afternoon when Julian came out of his gate. I side-skidded without meaning to and nearly came off. I asked him how his father was. He said, 'Daddy's fine. It's Mummy that isn't.' I asked him if he wanted to come out for a bike ride or anything and he said he didn't want to do anything much. I said, 'See you in the Christmas holidays, then.' He said 'Yes', and rode back down the drive.

I went down to Colin's and we read the new *Radio Fun* and mucked about with the tin telephone, but I didn't feel much like it and went back home. I really wanted to see Julian and go down to the camp and talk about things, but Daddy said he probably wanted to be alone with his parents, so I just mucked about at home and listened to 'Children's Hour'. It was a programme about Clackmannanshire which is in Scotland and is the smallest county in the British Isles. Mummy says it might come in useful one day. I can't imagine why.

Monday, December 17th

We had the school Carol Service this afternoon. We sang all the usual carols – 'Away in a Manger', 'Once in Royal David's', 'Hark the Herald', etc. The Lessons were read by a boy from each class. Raincock read the one about Mary and Joseph going to Bethlehem, and when it came to the bit about Mary being great with child, he got the giggles and had to be told to sit down. The chapel looked really nice for a change. Someone had stuck bits of holly on all the ledges, with candles instead of the usual lights.

The Chimp was reading the Lesson from St Luke about the man sent from God whose name was John, etc., and he'd just got to the bit about the true light that lighteth every man that cometh into the world when one of the candles fell over and set fire to the holly and Murch had to run and get a bucket of water. Unfortunately, when he was throwing the water onto the fire he missed and completely soaked Form II and they all had to go out and change.

Afterwards Seabrook went up to The Chimp and said it was really funny that it happened when it did and that Murch was a bit like John the Baptist in the River Jordan, baptising Form II. The Chimp said, 'All I can say, Seabrook, is that you've got a very peculiar sense of humour,' and he was made to stay behind and collect up all the hymn books, even though we were breaking up and Seabrook's parents had driven all the way from Sanderstead to collect him and had to sit outside in the car and wait until he'd finished.

Wednesday, December 19th

GRANNY Hodge has come to stay for Christmas. She's in a really happy mood now that Daddy's back. It must be really nice for her to be having Christmas with Daddy after all this time, though it's hard to think of him being someone's son.

In the afternoon we made paper chains by pasting strips of coloured paper together. Mummy made the paste by mixing flour and water and I found a brush from an old paint box for putting the paste on. Brock's had rationed the paper to one packet per family, but luckily Mummy had kept our chains from last year. They had got a bit crumpled in the loft and the paste had gone dry, so most of them had fallen apart, but Mrs Phipps was able to iron the ones that weren't too badly damaged and Granny and I re-pasted them so that they looked almost the same as the new ones.

While we were doing them, she told me about some of the films she's seen lately. One is *Anchors Aweigh* which is a musical with Gene Kelly and Frank Sinatra and Granny says is light-weight. Another is *The Body Snatchers* with Boris Karloff and Bela Lugosi. She made it sound so frightening that I didn't want to go up on my own to get undressed, and when I did I put all the lights on and searched every room before I had my bath.

Daddy came home earlier than usual, bringing some mistletoe which he hung under the light in the hall, and we all kissed each other under it, even Daddy and me, and Granny cried and then Mummy cried and Daddy said he thought a drink was in order, so we went into the drawing room and Daddy poured out drinks for everyone and we toasted each other and 'absent friends' and Granny let me have a sip of her sherry. It was even worse than a White Lady.

Because it was the first day of the holidays, and also because Mummy and Daddy both got a bit tiddly on gin, I was allowed to stay up and we listened to Big Bill Campbell and his Rocky Mountain Rhythm, and 'All the Old Log Cabin Favourites' – i.e., Buck Douglas, the Old Cowpunch; Peggy Bailey, the Sweet Voice of the West; Jakie Connolly, the Yodelling Cowboy; Ronnie Brolin and his Old Squeeze-box; and the Home Town Mountain Band. Personally I think it's one of the most boring programmes on the wireless, but Daddy likes it and I would like to like the things he likes, even if I don't.

Thursday, December 20th

I READ in the *Surrey Mirror* that Battle of Britain ace Archie Hill has been sent to prison for stealing a Tiger Moth from Biggin Hill and causing £100 worth of damage.

I said to Daddy that it didn't seem fair that one of The Few should be sent to prison when really he deserved a medal and Daddy said, 'The one thing you can be sure about in life, old man, is that nothing is fair.' I said that the Air Marshal told us the only thing you can be sure about in life is death. Daddy said, 'And that isn't always fair either.'

Friday, December 21st

I WAS going to go down and see Julian, but Mummy said he probably wanted to be alone with his father and that I should wait for him to get in touch with me. I was really fed up, but then Colin came round and we mucked about on our bikes and in the evening I went with him and his parents to the Plaza to see *Johnny Frenchman*. It was about these fishermen from Cornwall and Brittany in France, who are called Bretons, and there's a terrific rivalry between them, but then the Germans arrive and they become friends and work together against Hitler. The woman who was the skipper of the French boat was a real Frenchwoman with a real French accent. She's called Françoise Rosay and is very famous in France according to Mr Penwarden. Someone called Tom Walls was the Cornish harbourmaster. Mr Penwarden said he used to appear in funny plays in London before the war and that he was one of the funniest actors he'd ever seen. He didn't seem very funny to me.

During one of the scenes in Brittany, Colin suddenly said, 'That's Megavissey where we went on holiday last year.' Mrs Penwarden said, 'Mevagissey.' 'That's what I said,' he said. I said, 'Actually you said Megavissey, and it should be Mevagissey.' Colin said, 'How do you know? You've never been there.' A woman behind us started making shushing noises, but Colin got really batey and we nearly had a fight and the manageress came with her torch and said if we couldn't behave properly we'd have to leave. Mr Penwarden said, 'It's all right, they're with us.' The woman behind said, 'It's not all right. Can't you keep your children quiet? Some of us are trying to enjoy the film.'

Mr Penwarden said that actually only one of them was theirs, the other was a friend. She said she was surprised that anyone would allow their children to be taken out by people like them.

Everyone quietened down in the end, but in the excitement we had all lost the thread of the story so we left anyway and went back to the Penwardens' and had macaroni cheese and then I went home.

The really annoying thing about it was that when I got home I found I'd missed 'Merry-Go-Round'. *And* it was the Air Force edition, Much-Binding-in-the-Marsh.

I don't think I want to go out with the Penwardens again.

Saturday, December 22nd

Mrs Penwarden rang this morning and said would I like to go with them to the Oxted Players' Pantomime on January 13th. Last year I went with the Harringtons to *Cinderella*. Mr Soskice from the bank played one of the Ugly Sisters and was really funny and did an imitation of Old Mother Riley which was just like her, and his daughter Fay, who's sixteen, played Buttons and didn't wear a skirt, just stockings. Julian said it was a shame all boys didn't look like her and I said what about me and he said anything would be an improvement, and I wouldn't let him look at my programme.

This year it's *Dick Whittington*. Fay Soskice is playing Dick and her father is playing Dick's Mother. Mummy said I'd love to go, without asking me, and put the phone down.

I said that I thought I might be going with the Harringtons. She said, 'I don't think Peter Harrington will be feeling up to a pantomime after what he's been through.'

In the afternoon we drove over to the Wyndhams' at Merle Common and they gave us a small Christmas tree from their wood. Also a few eggs. After tea we got the box of decorations down from the loft. Some of the coloured balls were broken, but Mummy said we'd have to use them anyway and there wouldn't be any more where they came from for a long time.

The fairy is a little plastic doll in a pink dress with a very short flimsy skirt that sticks out all round and shows her legs. Granny says it's called tulle and it's usually used to make bridal veils. She looks a bit like Jill Pardoe – I mean the fairy, not Granny. I tried to imagine Jill dressed like that and couldn't.

Sunday, December 23rd

WE'VE had an invitation to a New Year's Eve party at the Masterson-Smiths'. It came with their Christmas card and had been delivered next door by mistake. On it was printed 'Mrs John Masterson-Smith At Home,' and written underneath was 'Bangers, Bubbly, Party Games and Dancing: 7.30 till late.' Our names were written across the top, and underneath someone – Anthony, I suppose – had written, 'Guy. Do come. It'll be fun. The Pardoes are coming and the Urquarts and Amanda and lots of other people you know.'

Granny said, 'That sounds fun. We always used to have a New Year's Eve party at home when I was a girl. I wish I was going.' Mummy said to me, 'Isn't Amanda Colin's cousin?' I said I wasn't sure, but I bet it's the same person, and that the only reason Anthony's asked her is to show off to me that he knows her, which he doesn't really. I probably won't go anyway. Mummy said, 'It's odd that Anthony seems to know who's going already. It can only mean they sent out the invitations ages ago and are only asking us at the last moment because a lot of people refused.'

Daddy said, 'Darling, don't be such a snob.' Mummy said, '*Me* a snob? I like that.' I said, 'What's a snob?' She said, 'Jean

Masterson-Smith's a snob.' I asked if we were snobs. 'Certainly not,' she said.

The Christmas 'Variety Bandbox' was on the Light Programme tonight. Derek Roy and Petula Clark were on. Funnily enough, she sounds a bit like Jill Pardoe. Ethel Revnell was on too, worst luck. I hate Ethel Revnell.

Monday, December 24th

CHRISTMAS Eve. Some more Christmas cards arrived. Two were robins on logs, two were stage-coaches going over bridges in the snow, and one was two partridges in the snow. My report came this afternoon by the second post. I bet The Chimp does it on purpose just to ruin everyone's Christmas.

My general reports weren't very good. Major Stanford-Dingley put 'Doesn't like rugger when it's wet and cold.' The Air Marshal said, 'A complete nonentity on the rugger field.' Mr Reader wrote, 'His rugger is decidedly on the feeble side. He must make up his mind to try harder and not think so much about the hard knocks.' The Chimp said, 'The liking for a muddy rugger ground and a kick on the shin will come in time. A Very Happy New Year to you all.'

I got 5 out of 10 for Character and 35 out of 120 for Special Effort, which I thought was a bit stingy considering how well I did in the boxing competition.

My worst subject was Maths. Stuffy Bedding wrote, 'I can't make up my mind whether he is a clever boy who derives some curious pleasure from pretending to be stupid, or just a very stupid boy. At all events, it is high time he braced up and put his back into it. Common Entrance looms and sitting at the back staring into space is not considered part of the curriculum.' For History, The Chimp put, 'Surprisingly vague.' Carpentry wasn't very good either. Mr Stapleford said, 'Give him the job and he will finish the tools.' Daddy thought that was frightfully funny. I didn't get it myself.

Luckily, Geography wasn't too bad. Major Stanford-Dingley said, 'A good term's work, though the sooner he learns to distinguish between Basutoland and Bechuanaland, the better his chances of putting up a decent mark on crop distribution in Southern Africa.'

For Latin, Gnasher put, 'He has worked well and I like his

enquiring turn of mind, but sometimes he rather overdoes it.'

All Daddy said was, 'Keep up the good work.' I was quite relieved.

After tea I wrote a letter to Father Christmas asking for a Stanley Gibbons stamp album like Peskett's, plus some stamps to stick in. As a P.S. I said I'd also like a cricket ball. Not a proper leather one, but one made of hard rubber with an imitation seam. Julian's got one and it looks quite realistic.

Mummy asked if she could check it through for spelling so I showed it to her and asked if I could have an envelope, but Mummy said that was a waste of paper and that it probably wouldn't go up the chimney anyway. So in the end I didn't even fold it. I waited till the flames had got going a bit and let it go and it disappeared just like that. Mummy said she hoped I wouldn't be disappointed if I didn't get exactly what I asked for and I said no, but secretly I will be.

I don't know if Colin or Julian believe in Father Christmas. I've never asked them and they've never talked about it. Wetherby-Brown says that anybody over the age of five who believes in him must want their brains tested. He said, 'If you honestly think that anyone can fly round the world in a sledge pulled by six reindeer and deliver presents to every single household in one night, you should be in the local loony bin.'

I reminded him that only the other day an RAF Meteor had flown at over 600 mph over Herne Bay and that it's only a matter of time before someone flies faster than the speed of sound. He said that RAF Meteors are not reindeer-driven, and that they haven't tried to land one on anyone's roof. Pilbrow said his father was in the RAF and he had a friend who did. We all asked what happened and Pilbrow said, 'He was killed and so was everyone in the house.'

Atwater says that everyone knows that people's parents stay up late on Christmas Eve, fiddling about in the kitchen and wrapping presents and having cherry brandy and getting spoony and when they're sure their children are asleep they put all the presents into the pillowcase and go to bed. Mackerel-Evans said, how come when he asks Father Christmas for something he always gets it? Atwater said because parents know what we're thinking all the time.

Holmes-Johnson said that's true, because whenever 'ITMA' is on in the evening and he asks if he can stay up and listen, before he can say more than two words, his mother says, 'I know what you're going to say and the answer is no.'

Anyway, I couldn't care less what other people think, especially Wetherby-Brown who's an idiot. All I know is that Mummy puts a pillowcase on the end of my bed before I go to sleep and always when I wake up it's got presents in it. I hope there is a Father Christmas, but even if there isn't, I really like doing the same things every year, like stirring the pudding and decorating the tree and sending a letter up the chimney, and this year it's better than ever, now that we're all together again.

Tuesday, December 25th

IT was pitch dark when I woke up. I put the light on. It was half-past one. I looked at the end of my bed and the pillowcase was still lying there empty. I tiptoed across and opened the door. There were no lights on anywhere, so I closed the door again, made sure my window catch was open and got back into bed. I lay awake for hours and hours, the whole night in fact, but no one came. At first I kept my eyes open, but as I couldn't see anything I closed them in the end and when I did open them soon afterwards, it was nearly light and my pillowcase had gone. I looked round and there it was, lying at the far end of my bed, all lumpy, just as usual. So, that proves Atwater is talking through his hat. I was awake all night and I never saw Daddy come in once. I never saw Father Christmas either for that matter, but that doesn't prove anything.

I have to admit it was odd that I didn't get the Stanley Gibbons stamp album I'd asked for, or the cricket ball, but I was very pleased with my Meccano set and I couldn't have cared less.

It's a No. 4 set and on the front of the box it shows a boy calling out and waving at a model of Tower Bridge. I can't imagine how you could possibly make Tower Bridge out of a No. 4 set. There aren't anything like enough pieces. Most are just straightforward lengths, but there are a few triangular pieces which must make the corners, and two boxes of nuts and bolts and washers plus two spanners, a screwdriver, a handle like the starting handle on our car, and quite a few wheels. Some have got rubber round the outside, but others are obviously meant to be used as pulleys because there are a couple of chains as well.

I also got a couple of copies of *Meccano Magazine*. One's got racing cars going round Brooklands on the front, the other shows a scene of the small airfield. Mummy and Daddy gave me the new *Radio Fun* Annual, which I really wanted. There are a lot of stories about Ethel Revnell which is a pity, but there are also quite a few about Stinker Murdoch, Tommy Handley and the ITMA gang, and Petula Clark. Only one about Issy Bonn and the Finkelfeffer Family, thank goodness. I can't wait to see Colin and show him.

I also got a little model field gun which fires matchsticks from Aunt Susan, Maureen and Milo, a wind-up Hornby  speedboat from Granny which I'm going to try out in the bath, a Conway Stewart Fountain Pen from Uncle Dick and Auntie Enid and all at Woodland Drive, some socks from Uncle Phil, Auntie Babs and Evelyn, two books from Grandpa and Grandma – *North After Seals*, which is about these people on this boat in Newfoundland going north after seals, and *Starlight* by H. Mortimer Batten which is the story of a timberwolf, and the usual five-shilling book token from Uncle Wilfred.

I started to make a crane with my Meccano, but had only managed to bolt two bits together when Mummy called out from her room and said, 'You can come in now.' I shoved everything into the pillowcase and went in. They were sitting up in bed having a cup of tea from the Teasmade. Daddy was wearing a brand-new bowler hat which looked very silly indeed with his striped pyjamas, and Mummy was wearing a woolly hat and gloves which looked even sillier.

They both said, 'Happy Christmas, tadpole,' and I jumped into the bed and we all hugged and kissed each other. I don't think I've ever felt happier in my life.

Then Mummy handed me a small package wrapped in rather crumpled red paper. I thought it was for me at first and then she said, 'Well, aren't you going to give Daddy his Christmas present?' So I did. It was a pair of garters. Daddy said, 'You obviously think I ought to pull my socks up,' and they both laughed. I didn't realise that was what I was giving him.

Then Daddy reached into his bedside table and got out another small package and said, 'And here's yours from Guy.' He gave it to me and I gave it to her. 'What *can* it be?' she said. Luckily I didn't know. It was a tub of Coty Foundation Cream, a box of Coty Airspun Face Powder, and a Coty Lipstick. '*Vif*,' she said. 'My favourite shade. Thank you, darling. How did you know?' And she gave me a kiss. 'I guessed,' I said. 'What a tactful boy,' she said.

After that I showed them all my presents. Daddy said, 'Meccano! I had a set when I was a boy. Actually, mine was a No. 5 Aeroplane Kit. But this is much better. You can make anything you like with this.' 'Tower Bridge?' I said pointing at the box. He said, 'Perhaps not straight away, but once you've got the hang of it, who knows?' Mummy said she was sorry I didn't get my stamp album, but perhaps I could have one for my birthday. I said I really didn't mind.

I wanted to ask her why all my other presents were in with Father Christmas's, but I didn't really want to know the answer.

Then we all went in to see Granny. She was very pleased with her bedjacket. When we were alone, I said, 'Your present came with Father Christmas's.' She said, 'What did you expect? A special delivery?'

After breakfast we all went to church. It was very cold out. Mummy made me take my coat and scarf off when we got in. She said if I didn't I wouldn't feel the benefit.

I didn't mind the carols, but the sermon went on for weeks. I can't remember what it was about because I was thinking about how to make Tower Bridge out of my Meccano set and wasn't really listening.

We bumped into the Masterson-Smiths on the way out. Daddy said, 'Happy Christmas, Colonel,' with special emphasis on the 'Colonel', and gave me a huge wink. Mr Masterson-Smith said, 'And the compliments of the season to you too, Robin.' Mrs Masterson-Smith said, 'I hope you're all coming to our party on New Year's Eve.' Mummy said, 'We'd love to and we promise that if we have to drop out for any reason, we'll let you know in plenty of time so you can make the numbers up.'

Anthony said, 'I'm glad Amanda's coming.' I said, 'So am I.' He said, 'I thought you would be,' and gave me what was meant to be a smile, but looked as if he was about to be sick.

We had Christmas lunch in the dining room. Mummy had decorated the table by putting a long piece of red crêpe paper down the middle and a white piece on the top and some sprigs of holly and macrocarpa and, right in the middle, a mirror with little figures on it and cotton wool piled up round the sides so that it looked like a frozen lake with people skating on it. It was very realistic.

As Daddy was carving the chicken, he said, 'We'll have a turkey next year, I promise. There'll be more of everything by then.'

Actually, having seen the Wyndhams' turkeys close to I was quite glad we were on starvation rations, as Daddy put it. Granny was very keen to have the parson's nose. Rather her than me, when you think where it goes on a chicken.

Mummy and Daddy drank a bottle of red wine which looked quite nice but smelt disgusting. I had some Tizer and Granny had a glass of Wincarnis. She winked at me and said, 'For my wind, dear.'

I had forgotten Mummy had put silver threepenny bits in the Christmas pudding and I think I swallowed one. Granny said, 'That's meant to be good luck.' She always says that when something goes wrong. I asked how was I going to get it out and Mummy said, 'Don't worry. Nature will take its course.' But how do you not worry when something like that happens? Supposing it gets stuck half-way down? Or, worse still, right inside somewhere, and goes green like the teaspoons do sometimes, and I get poisoned and die? Colin's *Wonder Book of Science* may have something about it, but I won't be able to see him till tomorrow. Funnily enough, I've got a bit of a tummy pain. Granny says that's because I've eaten too much, but I'm not so sure.

At two o'clock Daddy turned on the Home Service. He said it was to make sure the set was warmed up in time for the King's Broadcast to the Empire at three, but personally I think it was because he was a bit bored. I certainly was, after listening to what was on. It was called 'Wherever You May Be' and it was different people describing what Christmas is like in different places – on a minesweeper, in a Services Hospital, on the SS *Queen Elizabeth*, in Prague and Oslo, etc. All I can say is, I'm glad I was in Fernhurst Road.

When the King came on they played the National Anthem and Daddy made us all stand to attention. I can't remember what the King said now, but I remember thinking his voice was gruffer than ever. After he had wished us all a Happy Christmas they played the National anthem and we all had to stand to attention again, and Granny's handbag fell off her lap onto the floor and powder went everywhere.

After we'd done the washing-up, the grown-ups went into the drawing room and fell asleep in front of the fire and I stayed in the morning room and tried to make a little man with my Meccano set. I did everything it said in the instruction book, using the wheels for eyes, etc., but the thing I finished up with didn't look like anything human, though funnily enough it did look quite like Chimp Harris.

The worst thing about Meccano is that although you're supposed to hold the nut with the spanner while you tighten the bolt with the screwdriver, there usually isn't enough room to get the spanner in, so you either have bolts sticking out all over the place or else you have to press your finger hard against the nut to stop it going round. I did the latter and now my left finger is really sore.

Luckily my tummy pain has gone, but I still haven't forgotten about the silver threepenny bit. I don't know which worries me more, that or my sore finger.

At half-past four Mummy went out and got tea ready. She had made a small fruit cake with white icing and had decorated it with some more figures – a robin on a log, a polar bear, a little angel, etc. – and a sprig of holly. I helped her push it in on the trolley, but the wheels went funny and we nearly crashed into the Christmas tree.

I had two pieces of cake, not because I was that hungry but I thought it might help to push the threepenny bit through.

'Children's Hour' was even more boring than 'Wherever You May Be'. Children with foreign accents came on and sent Christmas greetings from places like France, Denmark, Holland, Czechoslovakia, Russia and Austria and sang foreign carols which weren't nearly as good as ours. In fact the more foreign people I hear on the wireless, the more glad I am that I'm English.

After that there was a special Christmas edition of 'Regional Round' with Uncle Mac. I don't know why he's called Uncle. He always sounds grumpy, and I can't imagine anyone wanting to have an uncle like that. Perhaps he thinks if he calls himself Uncle it will make him seem more kindly.

We didn't do much for the rest of the day. In fact I was quite glad when it was time to go to bed. I have started reading *Starlight*. I thought I could hear a wolf howling in the woods. It's cold enough for wolves.

Wednesday, December 26th

I STARTED to make a windmill with my Meccano this morning and had finished the base when Mummy came in and said I hadn't forgotten we were going at half-past nine, had I, and had I cleaned my teeth yet, and would I get a clean hanky from the bottom drawer, and I wasn't going to go out with my hair like that, was I?

When I asked where we were going, she told me not to be sillier than I needed and that I knew very well we were going to Uncle Dick and Auntie Enid's in Purley for lunch. I said did I have to, I was thinking of going down to Colin's and showing him my *Radio Fun* Annual, and Mummy said of course I had to, Grandma and Grandpa were going to be there, Uncle Dick was collecting them from Coulsdon, and Uncle Phil and Auntie Babs were coming over from Banstead for tea. I said, 'And Evelyn?' She said, 'Evelyn is twenty-six. She is a law unto herself.'

Actually, I don't mind Uncle Dick, except when he does his ITMA imitations, and Roland and Denis are okay except that all they ever want to do is play New Footy and I've never really trusted Denis ever since I went to stay with them for a week and he tried to get me to do peculiar things in the bath. Mummy says I should be nicer to them, considering that most of my clothes have been handed down by them. I knew my pullover was hand-knitted but not even Mummy could have gone such a mucker round the neck. Also the aertex shirts smell really odd.

Woodland Drive where they live is really steep and as they live right at the top Daddy had to take a run at it and even then we jolly nearly didn't make it. As it was, we had to turn round and face the other way and put bricks under the wheels in case the brakes weren't strong enough. Uncle Dick said that some friends of theirs had driven up from East Grinstead once and run out of steam half-way up and rolled all the way back down to the bottom. Daddy said, 'Were they all right?' Uncle Dick said, 'No, they ruddy well weren't.'

Grandma and Grandpa were sitting by the fire having a glass of Dry Fly sherry when we arrived. Grandma said, 'Hallo, you're a big boy.' She always says the same thing. So does Grandpa. He shakes me by the hand and says, 'How's school?' and I always say, 'Not too bad, thank you,' and he says, 'That's the ticket. Bash on. Remember, you can only do your best.'

Denis and Roland wanted to have a game of New Footy as soon as I got there. They'd laid an old brown army blanket out on the table in the morning room and marked out the lines with chalk and the players were all in position ready for the kick-off. One team wore blue and white and the other wore red and white. They're only cut out of cardboard and glued onto buttons which you flick with your finger to make them move, but they all look as if they're running so they're quite realistic, which is more than can be said for the goalposts which are made of wire and have paper netting stuck on the back.

Denis and I played first. Roland was the referee and had a shiny whistle with a pea in it which he blew for the kick-off. Denis immediately scored a goal. Roland said, 'Hard cheese,' and was replacing the figures when Uncle Dick came in and said it was lunchtime. Denis said couldn't we just have one more go and Uncle Dick said, 'You've got all afternoon to play.' I don't know which made me feel more fed up, the thought of playing New Footy all afternoon, or the lunch. Auntie Enid said it was chicken fricassée, but it looked to me exactly like the chicken-in-sick we have at school. The greens from the garden were all watery, so were the mashed potatoes. Actually, I think school food is better. There was Christmas pudding again, but no silver threepenny bits, thank goodness. I looked this morning but there was no sign of the one I swallowed yesterday.

We had crackers with the pudding. Mine didn't go off. There were tiny plastic charms inside. I had a bell. My motto said, 'A stitch in time saves nine.' Grandpa said, 'Very good advice. It certainly saved a lot of men's bacon in the trenches.' The paper hats were the thinnest I've ever seen. Mine tore as I was putting it on, but I wore it anyway.

After that Grandpa and Daddy lit their pipes and all the rest of the grown-ups had cigarettes and Uncle Dick brought round a bottle of ruby red port. Daddy said, 'How did you manage to get your hands on that?' Uncle tapped the side of his nose. Denis and Roland were allowed a small sip of port each, so I was too. I thought it tasted quite nice. A bit like cough mixture, but sweeter.

Daddy said, 'Have you been listening to "ITMA" lately?' Uncle Dick said, 'Yes, but I've given up doing my imitations.' Mummy said, 'Oh, what a shame.' Uncle said, 'Yes, I've moved onto "Much-Binding-in-the-Marsh" now,' and he started doing imitations of Stinker Murdoch and Sam Costa. They were even worse than his ones of Tommy Handley and Jack Train.

After lunch Grandma and Grandpa had forty winks in front of the fire and the rest of us were made to go for a walk in the nearby woods while Mummy and Auntie Enid washed up and got tea ready. Roland found a huge pine cone in the woods and said, 'Let's have a game of football.' They won 15–3.

We got back just as Uncle Phil and Auntie Babs were arriving. They were both very jolly and said, 'Goodness, you've grown.' Evelyn looked grumpy, as usual, and sat in a corner smoking and wouldn't speak to anyone. Auntie Babs said, 'Don't take any notice of her. She's in love.' When I asked who with, Evelyn said, 'It's none of your business.'

Auntie Babs said, 'He's called Mario.' Evelyn said, 'Franco. How many more times do I have to tell you? His name's Franco.' Auntie Babs said, 'Mario, Franco, it's all one to me.' Uncle Phil said, 'He was a prisoner-of-war in Scotland, now he works as a mechanic in the local garage.' Uncle Dick said, 'A grease-monkey, eh?' Evelyn burst into tears and rushed out of the room. Mummy said, 'Tact, Richard.' Uncle Dick said, 'What's wrong with that? It's what they call garage mechanics in America.' Mummy said, 'Well, we're not in America now, we're in Purley.'

Uncle Phil said, 'He's done wonders with the gearbox on my Standard Eight.' Daddy said, 'He doesn't seem to have done such a good job with Evelyn.' Auntie Enid said, 'I'll go and talk to her. She'll be all right.' But she obviously wasn't, because Auntie Enid came back alone. She looked at me and said, 'You've got all this to come.' I don't know what she could possibly have meant. I'm not going to work in a garage, I'm not an Italian, and, if I was, I wouldn't go out with someone like Evelyn. She looks just like Anna May Wong but without the slitty eyes.

The Banstead Brigade, as Daddy calls them, said they had to get back to feed the cat and left soon after tea. I didn't see Evelyn, but I suppose she went with them. If that's what being in love with someone's like, I don't think I'll bother. In fact, I probably won't go to the Masterson-Smiths' after all. I couldn't care less if Amanda goes or not.

Denis and Roland tried to get another game of New Footy going, but Daddy said he thought we ought to be on our way before the roads turned nasty. I felt like saying 'Before Denis and Roland turn nasty, more likely.'

We skidded twice on the way home. When we got in, there was a small parcel lying beside the front door, addressed to me. It was some playing cards and a little book called *How to Play Canasta*. There was no card inside.

Daddy said, 'Who on earth could that be from?' I looked at Mummy, but she didn't say anything. I said, 'It might be from Julian.' Daddy said, 'Hm.'

I finished my windmill after supper. I followed the instructions very carefully, but it still looked nothing like the picture. I'll probably try something a bit easier next time, like a table.

As I was getting ready for bed, I said quietly to Mummy, 'Do you think Uncle Bob sent those cards?' She said, 'Yes.' I said I did, too. She said, 'He's very fond of you, you know.' I said I liked him, too. She said, 'He's a very nice man.' I said, 'So he isn't in South Africa, then?' She said, 'No.' I said, 'Was that him I saw in Oxted the other day?' She said, 'More than likely.' I said, 'Have you seen him?' She said, 'No.' I said, 'Are you going to see him?' She said, 'That wouldn't be very fair on Daddy, would it?' 'I suppose not,' I said.

Thursday, December 27th

I woke up just before seven and it was almost light. I pulled back the curtains. It was snowing hard and the whole garden was covered with a thick white blanket, with only lumps and bumps to show where everything was.

I got up straight away and went out and made a snowman, using lumps of coal for eyes and a carrot for the nose. It looked just like Chimp Harris. Everything I make ends up looking like him.

After breakfast we got the toboggan out. It isn't a very good one. Worms made it for me last year out of old bits of wood. He said they fell off the back of a lorry. It was jolly lucky he happened to be going by at the time. It doesn't have any proper metal along the bottom of the runners or anything, but if you rub some candlewax on, it goes quite fast, especially when everybody's been up and down a few times.

It stopped snowing at about ten and we got to Oakwood Meadow at about half-past. Everyone was there – the Penwardens, the Pardoes, the Urquarts, the Masterson-Smiths – so the snow was quite well flattened and some toboggans were already going almost to the stream at the bottom.

My first go was a bit slow but we rubbed some more wax on and Daddy had a go and beat Dickie Pargeter easily. Then I had another go and beat Anthony Masterson-Smith and his nanny, Betty, even though his toboggan is huge compared with mine and has metal runners. He and Betty always go down on it together, both sitting upright, with him at the front and her behind. (Actually, that's quite a good joke, seeing how fat she is. Daddy says that the more weight you carry, the faster you go, but, as Gnasher says, there are exceptions to every rule.)

Colin had brought his racing toboggan, as usual. It's got a wooden seat, but the runners are completely made of metal. Colin says it's called a skeleton. The best thing about it, apart from the fact that it goes like a rocket, is that it has a bar across the front for steering. It's attached to the runners and when you turn it, it twists the runners to the right or left. It really works.

Colin and I raced each other twice and he won by miles both times. Then we did a swop, but he won again on mine anyway. Then Daddy and Mr Penwarden had a race. Mr Penwarden was miles ahead, but he got a coughing fit and fell off.

After a while Mummy came up with a basket with biscuits and a thermos of hot Bovril. It didn't taste anything like the stuff we have at school and I had two mugs of it.

Mummy said, 'Who on earth's that?' and she pointed to the

far side of the field where two people were going down on skis. Daddy said, 'I can't see from here, but they've certainly raised the tone of the occasion.' Mrs Masterson-Smith said, 'Shown us all up, more likely.'

Suddenly, Julian appeared from nowhere pulling a small wooden toboggan. I said, 'Where did you get that from?' He said, 'My grandmother bought it in Switzerland. She used to go tobogganing there every year. Davos, usually.'

Daddy said, 'How's your father getting on?' Julian said, 'Fine, thank you, sir, considering he hasn't put on a pair of skis for seven years.' He said to me, 'Race you later? I must go and talk to my parents first.'

When he was out of earshot, Mummy said, 'What on earth does Peter think he's doing on skis?'

'Trying to ski,' said Daddy.

'And not making a very good job of it,' said Mrs Masterson-Smith.

We saw Julian talking to them and they both waved and Mrs Harrington started walking towards us on her skis. She was really out of breath when she got to us.

Mummy said, 'Is Peter all right?' She sounded quite worried. Mrs Harrington said, 'Oh, he's loving every minute of it. We're both a bit rusty, of course. Not surprising really, considering we haven't been near the slopes since we went to Wengen in 1938, but we'll soon get our ski legs back.'

Daddy said, 'What Daphne means is, isn't it a bit soon to be taking so much violent exercise? I mean, after what he's been through with the Japs, shouldn't he be at home trying to get his strength back?' Mrs Harrington said, 'Oh, dear. What has Julian been telling you now? The fact is, he was only in the prison for three weeks before they were all let out, so he didn't come to a lot of harm, unlike some.' Mummy said, 'But he's so dreadfully thin.' Mrs Harrington said, 'They all are. There's even less to eat in the jungle than there is here.' Daddy said, 'But he was on a stick when I last saw him.' 'Oh, that,' she said. 'The silly chump slipped as he was coming down the gangway and twisted his ankle. He's fine now.'

As we were leaving for lunch, Mummy said to Daddy, 'Some people live in a different world from us.' Julian certainly does.

DADDY went up to London today and I went tobogganing in the afternoon with Colin and Julian. Rory Urquart was there with a tin tray and his sister Lettice. He's all right, but she goes pink as soon as anyone speaks to her and never says a word. When I told Mummy this, she said, 'She should have very little difficulty finding a husband.' Eleven seems very young to be getting married.

Anyway, we had good fun. The main track is much faster now that the snow has been completely flattened. We made a jump in the middle and Rory took off and he and his tray went all the way to the bottom separately. In fact, he got there before the tray. Colin went so fast once that he actually jumped the stream. Julian tried and went straight in.

It was almost dark when we all went home. I asked Lettice if she was going to the Masterson-Smiths' party and I thought she was going to burst into tears. Mummy said, 'You've got to be polite when you speak to girls.' I said I was. She said, not polite enough, apparently. I don't know why I bother. I don't really want to talk to them. I only spoke to Lettice out of politeness in the first place.

I was in the middle of listening to L. Hugh Newman talking on 'Nature Parliament' about grey squirrels and how one day there might be more of them than the red ones, when Mummy came in and said she wanted to talk about something, so I switched it off. It wasn't very interesting anyway, or very likely.

She said, 'You do like Julian, don't you?' I said of course. She said, 'Would you say he was your best friend?' I said, 'One of.' She said, 'Do you think he's a bit of a fibber?' I said, 'A bit.' She said, 'Do you mind?' I said, 'Not specially.' She said, 'You don't like him less because he fibs sometimes?' I said, 'Not really.' She said, 'Not all fibs are necessarily bad. I mean, if someone deliberately told a fib in order to prevent someone else from being hurt, for example, it would be a good thing to fib, wouldn't you agree?' I said, 'I suppose so.' She said, 'Do you know what I'm talking about?' I said not really. She said it was probably just as well and that I should go to bed and forget all about it, so I did, but I haven't forgotten about it. In fact, I've been thinking about it quite a lot. The trouble is, I still don't know what she was talking about.

JANUARY

I WENT to the Masterson-Smiths' party after all. At first I wished I hadn't. Mummy and Daddy went off to the drawing room to have drinks with the other grown-ups and I was left standing in the hall wondering what to do when Anthony stuck his head out from another room and said, 'We're all in here.' I went in expecting to see lots of people but there was no one else there at all. All the furniture had been pushed up against the wall and the carpet had been rolled back. Anthony gave me a drink which tasted pink. I asked him if anyone else was coming. 'Of course,' he said. 'Why shouldn't they be?' I said, 'No reason. How about Amanda?' 'Of course,' he said. 'Do you know her?' I pretended I did. 'Grand girl,' he said. 'Yes,' I said. Then a whole lot of people arrived and Anthony rushed off into the hall to meet them.

As each person came into the room, Anthony stuck a label on their back with the name of half of a famous couple on it, such as Adam, or Judy, or Worzel Gummidge, or somebody, and we all had to go round asking people questions to try and find out if we were their other half. Once we had found our partner we had to take them into the other room and have supper with them.

I don't know why we couldn't just ask someone we knew already or had come with. It would have been much easier, but Anthony said it was more fun this way. But it wasn't, because we had never heard of half the names, so we took weeks trying to find each other and everyone got frightfully fed up. A girl who looked really nice, with long hair, came over and said, 'Hallo, you're David.' I said I was Guy, actually. She said, 'I meant the name on your back. It's David.' I felt a bit of a fool and went red but she didn't seem to mind and said, 'Oh dear,

I've given the game away.' I said it didn't matter. She said she'd been there for ages and had asked everybody thousands of questions, but she still couldn't work out who she was and she was getting really hungry. I thought I wouldn't mind having supper with her and said had she thought of asking somebody 'Who am I?' and she said no and asked me. I was just going to tell her when Anthony came over and said, 'We've stopped playing now. I'm Robin Hood and Amanda here is Maid Marian. Come on, let's have supper, I'm starved,' and he led her out of the room. I couldn't believe it. To make matters worse, I found that Bathsheba was Lettice Urquart.

I tried talking to Lettice at supper, but it was a complete waste of time as all she ever said was 'Yes' and 'No', and I had to give up and pretend I wasn't feeling very well and went to the lavatory and sat there for a bit wishing I really *was* ill so I could go home. After a while it got really cold in there with my trousers down, so I went back in. Luckily, Lettice was talking to her brother, so I went to talk to Amanda. I said I liked her bracelet. She said, 'I got it off a jar of potted meat.' At that moment Anthony turned up and said, 'Sorry, Guy, Amanda's *my* partner for supper,' and gave me one of his sickly smiles. I wish he was my opponent for the House Boxing Competition.

We were having jellies in little white cardboard bowls when Mrs Masterson-Smith put her head round the door and said, 'Everything going all right in here?' Everyone said, 'Yes, thank you, Mrs Masterson-Smith,' but I didn't say anything.

After supper we all had to go back into the 'night-club', as Anthony called it, and he got out his wind-up gramophone and made us do something called a Paul Jones. All the girls had to stand in a ring facing outwards and all the boys had to stand in a ring outside facing the girls. Then we all had to hold hands and when the music started the two rings moved round in opposite directions and when it stopped you had to dance with the person opposite you.

The first time I got Barbara Kippax, which wasn't too bad. The song on the gramophone was 'Chickery Chick' and we just mucked about trying to remember the words. I noticed her lips were very red and asked her if she was wearing lipstick. She said sort of. When I asked her what she meant, she said it wasn't real lipstick, she'd done it with a boiled sweet, lots of the girls did.

The second time I got a girl with such a big plate in her mouth with huge wires across her teeth that I could hardly understand a word she said. I tried asking her about boiled sweets but there was no point. The song was 'Don't Fence Me In'.

I said, 'This is quite a suitable song, considering your plate.' She said, 'I don't think that's at all funny,' and walked off. The next time I pulled and pushed the people next to me to make sure I'd be opposite Amanda when the music stopped. When it did I was, and I was just going to say hallo when Anthony pushed in and said, 'I forgot to mention, this is an Excuse Me,' and he grabbed hold of Amanda and somehow I finished up with Lettice Urquart again.

I tried my best to copy Anthony, but we kept treading on each other's feet and suddenly Lettice said in a loud voice, 'I'll be boy now,' and before I knew what, *I* was being pushed round the floor like Amanda. I hoped she hadn't seen, but she had. She was laughing, and I honestly don't think it was because of anything Anthony said. To make matters worse, the tune on the record was 'Kiss Me Once and Kiss Me Twice and Kiss Me Once Again, It's Been a Long, Long Time'. I didn't feel like kissing Lettice once, and certainly not twice. I could see her looking at me in a funny way as if she hoped I would, but I pretended I hadn't noticed.

After the Paul Jones we played a few more games and then we played Sardines. Lettice went off to hide first. Then Julian went off, then Jill Pardoe, then Rory Urquart, then Amanda, then Anthony, then Barbara Kippax, then me.

I was upstairs when I found a little staircase that led to another floor. I went up and turned on the light, but it had a blackout bulb and I could hardly see anything. I came to a door and opened it and went in. It looked like a bedroom. It was freezing cold and completely dark and I was about to shut the door again when I heard a girl's voice saying, 'Who's that?' I said who it was. She said, 'Oh good, I'm in here.' 'Where?' I said. 'Over here, next to the bed,' she said. I went to look but I still couldn't see anything. 'In this

cupboard,' she said. I suddenly realised it sounded a bit like Lettice Urquart and I was just saying something like 'Actually we're just going,' when suddenly a hand came out from nowhere and grabbed me by the arm and pulled me into this tiny cupboard.

I said, 'Is that you, Lettice?' 'No,' she said. I said, 'Who is it, then?' She said, 'Guess.' I said I couldn't and asked who else was in there. 'No one,' she said. 'Just us.' I said it was freezing in there. She said, 'There are these blankets. We can wrap ourselves in them.'

We did, and sat there for a bit. After a while I said, 'Shouldn't we go down and try and find the others?' She said, 'What for?' I said I thought the whole point of Sardines was that everybody finished up in the same place. She said, 'I thought this was the whole idea of Sardines,' and before I knew what, I was being kissed on my face.

I've only ever been kissed by Mummy before, and Granny, of course, and once by Auntie Susan, and I've often wondered what it would be like to be kissed by a girl. It's really nice, actually. It makes you feel quite tingly, not in a tickly sort of way so you want it to stop, but in a nice way so that you don't.

After she'd kissed me a couple of times, she said, 'You can kiss me now if you want.' I felt really peculiar, as if I was in a dream and any moment I would wake up, but I didn't, so I leaned forward and kissed her. Actually, I didn't because it was so dark I couldn't see her and kissed a bit of blanket by mistake, but then I worked out where she was and it went quite well the second time. She said, 'If you like, I could kiss you on the lips like they do in the films.' I said, 'All right,' and that was even better than being kissed on the cheek. Then I tried it and that was nice too.

Suddenly we heard someone coming down the passage. The door of the bedroom opened. She put her hand over my mouth and said 'Ssh' very quietly, and Anthony's voice called out, 'Amanda? Are you in there?' Then he closed the door and walked off down the passage.

I said, 'Are you Amanda?' She said, 'Yes.' I said, 'Are you Colin's cousin?' She said, 'Yes' again. I said, 'I'm Guy.' She said, 'I know.'

We were in there for ages. When we came downstairs, everyone was with the grown-ups and the wireless was on and when Big Ben chimed twelve, everyone cheered and kissed each other. Mrs Pardoe was kissing Mr Henriksen in a film star sort of way. Mummy came across and said, 'Happy New Year, tadpole,' and kissed me. I looked at Amanda to see if she was giggling, but she wasn't. None of the children kissed each other so I didn't kiss Amanda. Anthony was on the other side of the room. He was obviously in quite a bate. Then suddenly Lettice Urquart came up and kissed him. He leapt away as if he'd been electrocuted. Then he saw Amanda and started to come across and, as he did, I kissed her right on the lips. His mouth literally fell open and I winked at him.

Daddy came up and ruffled my hair and said, 'Happy New Year, old man.' I said, 'Yes.'

I'm really looking forward to 1946, except that I'm really tired this morning and I've got a bit of a headache. Also, there's still no sign of my silver threepenny bit.

Wednesday, January 2nd

THEY'VE just started doing test flights from a place near London I've never heard of. It isn't an airport or anything, just a few huts and tents and a runway, but apparently it might be one day. It's called Heath Row.

The first test flight was to Montevideo. It's a funny place to choose, but I suppose they've got to go somewhere.

Thursday, January 3rd

ACCORDING to the *Daily Express*, another copy of Hitler's will has been found in a place called Dortmund and people are beginning to wonder if he really is dead after all. Actually, Julian thought he saw someone looking just like Hitler coming out of Boots the other day. I said, 'Did he have a little moustache?' and Julian said, 'Of course he did. He wouldn't have looked like Hitler otherwise, would he?'

Wednesday, January 9th

GOERING and Ribbentrop went on trial yesterday. According to Mrs Phipps, Goering used to dress up in women's clothes. I can't imagine why he should want to do a thing like that.

There's a picture of him in a *Lilliput* Annual that I found on a shelf in the drawing room. On one side of the page there's Goering with his mouth open going 'Blur . . . blur . . . blur . . . blur . . . blur . . .' and on the other side there's Mr Hore-Belisha with his mouth shut saying 'Poof!' It's really funny the way they put these photographs opposite each other, like showing the tops of a lot of bald heads on one side and a plate of fried eggs on the other, or Monsieur Bonnet the French Foreign Minister on one side and a salmon-breasted cockatoo looking just like him on the other. I don't read the articles much, but I do like the lists of facts, like the one that tells you how much everything in the war cost, e.g., a 1,090-ton submarine cost £349,750, a service rifle cost £8 and a gas mask cost 2*s* 6*d*. They also have some quite good cartoons sometimes, like the man and the woman in the chemist's and the woman hasn't got a head and the man's saying, 'We've come about the vanishing cream.'

The thing I like best about *Lilliput*, though, are the bare women. They have them all the time and they're really really bare, without any clothes on at all. You can't see everything, but what you can see is jolly good and anyway, you can imagine the rest. Well, Julian can, and I think I can. I haven't asked Colin. There's one I especially like which has a tank roaring up a hill and underneath it says 'Tank trap' and opposite is this bare woman who is lying flat out on the grass covered with netting. There's another one I like, too, which shows a bare lady running across a beach saying 'See you next summer.' I wouldn't mind seeing her next summer. Daddy said they were put there to cheer up the soldiers who were far from home. They certainly cheer me and Colin up.

Friday, January 11th

I WOKE up in the middle of the night and I was so cold I had to put my vest and dressing gown on *in bed*. And I've got chilblains on my hands and feet. They itch like anything, especially at night. In fact, that's probably one of the reasons I woke up. Mummy says it comes from getting my feet frozen in the snow and putting them straight into hot water when I come in. But how else am I going to thaw them out? The radiators are hardly warm at all and we used up most of the coal ration at Christmas. We've got a stone hot-water bottle, but I'm only allowed to have it for a bit and then Mummy takes it away and puts it in their bed. I said why didn't we buy another, but she says they're in short supply. I said that everything seemed to be in short supply. She said, 'I know. It's just like being in the war all over again, but much less fun.'

Mr Churchill has gone off on a holiday to Florida. I don't blame him.

Sunday, January 13th

LAST night I went to the Barn Theatre with the Penwardens to see *Dick Whittington*. Amanda came too and I sat next to her and held her hand. Anthony was there with his parents and the Urquarts. I noticed he was not sitting next to Lettice.

It was the best pantomime I've ever seen, not that I've seen many, apart from *Cinderella*. The Form IVs did *Jack and the Beanstalk* the Christmas before last. It was quite good, especially when Jack who was played by McGurk pretended to cut down the beanstalk and it fell over and Ibbotson and Hebblethwaite were standing there trying to change their costumes wearing only their underpants. The Chimp acted the part of the Ogre. Wetherby-Brown said, 'He didn't have to do much acting.'

Dick Whittington was much better than that, though, with proper scenery and costumes and really good acting – especially by Mr Soskice who wore an orange wig and lots of make-up and huge false bosoms and did a really funny dance with Dick's cat. The best bit was when the two brokers' men were trying to nail two bits of wood together and they handed Dick's mother the hammer and one of them said, 'When I nod my head, you hit it,' and instead of hitting the nail she hit his head.

Fay Soskice's legs were even longer than last year. Just as they were changing the scenery for the last scene, the Prince's Palace, Colin said, 'I'm thinking of marrying Fay one day, actually.' I asked him if he knew her. 'No,' he said, 'but I will when I marry her.' I wanted to say I was going to marry Amanda, but I didn't have a chance because the band suddenly started up and the curtain opened and the whole cast sang 'We're Riding Along on the Crest of a Wave'.

I wouldn't at all mind being an actor. A film star, preferably, like Ronald Colman, but if not, then in pantomimes.

Monday, January 14th

G OING to the Pictures was on 'Children's Hour'. It tells you about the films that are on that children might like to see. *Midnight Raiders* with Tex Ritter doesn't sound very good, but I might go and see *Abbott and Costello in Hollywood*. The ones that I'm really looking forward to next month are *The Bandit of Sherwood Forest* with Cornel Wilde, and *Tarzan and the Leopard Woman*. With a bit of luck I might pick up some swimming tips from Johnny Weissmuller.

Wednesday, January 16th

I WASN'T able to write my journal yesterday because I was in London all day with Daddy. We caught the 8.03. The platform was quite crowded and we had to push our way past lots of men wearing bowler hats and carrying umbrellas and reading the *Daily Telegraph*.

I said why didn't we just get on anywhere? Daddy explained that he always travelled up with the same people in the same compartment near the back of the train and that the ones who get on at earlier stations like Hurst Green Halt always keep a place for him. I said what about me and he said David Bascombe was away and they had agreed that I could sit in his place. I asked who all these people were and Daddy said, 'Army chums mainly.'

Dickie Pargeter arrived just after we did, and Atwater's father, and Holmes-Johnson's father. When the train pulled in, Dickie stepped forward and opened the door and we all got in. I thought it was going to be an ordinary compartment, but it was just like a small sitting room with tables and armchairs. You could hardly see across the other side for the cigarette smoke.

We all sat down and Daddy introduced me to everyone. There was one empty place. Dickie said, 'Hallo, somebody else on MO's report?' One of the men who was already there said, 'Bob Tremayne's got Delhi Belly. Says he picked it up in Ooty.' One of the others said, 'Not the only thing he picked up in India, I'm told.' Everyone laughed. One of them said, 'Too many cherry brandies in the pub last night, if you ask me,' and they all laughed again, and I did too.

The guard had just blown his whistle when the door opened and a man jumped in and tried to sit in the empty seat. Dickie Pargeter said, 'Sorry, chum, that one's taken,' so the man had to get off again and try another compartment. I saw him running along the platform, but by that time the train had started to move and he missed it. As we went by him, I suddenly realised it was Uncle Bob. I don't know if he recognised me or not but I felt myself go red. I don't think Daddy realised who it was.

After a bit I asked him why they pretended the seat was taken when it wasn't. Dickie Pargeter said, 'Good God, we don't want to have to sit with people we don't know.'

Mr Holmes-Johnson put his newspaper down and said, 'Do you remember the time that chap got on and sat down and refused to leave?' One of the others said, 'And you set fire to his newspaper before we'd even got to the tunnel.' And everyone roared with laughter again.

We were just pulling out of Riddlesdown Station when Holmes-Johnson's father looked up from his newspaper and said, 'I see in the Births column of the *Daily Telegraph* that a Mrs Jones of Oxshott has given birth to laughter. This is either a misprint, or someone has been poking fun at her.' I have never seen grown-ups laugh so much. I didn't get it at all and when I said so, they laughed even louder.

Later on they all stopped reading their newspapers and Dickie Pargeter got out a pack of cards and they started playing bridge. Daddy said to me, 'Not a word of this to Mummy, mind.'

When we got off at London Bridge, Daddy and I caught a bus to his office.

Unfortunately, I couldn't see out properly because the window next to me was covered in scratches. The conductor said that was because of scraping off the anti-blast netting. He said, 'Think yourself lucky, sunshine. In the war you'd have had just a diamond-shaped hole to look through.'

Daddy's office wasn't very interesting, so I went out for a walk. I didn't realise how much of the City had been bombed. St Paul's is still there, of course, and the Mansion House and the Bank of England, but there are whole bits which have been roped off and are nothing but piles of bricks and earth.

For lunch we went to a sandwich bar next to Liverpool Street Station. We sat on a stool at a counter and had a cheese sandwich each and Daddy had tea and I had nothing. There were a lot of other people in there looking like the ones on the train. Then we went next door to have our hair cut at a barber's called Katte's. It was much better than Mr Ellis's in Limpsfield High Street. For one thing there were proper chairs with black leather and shiny metal, and a mirror to look into.

Daddy had his hair cut first, though it didn't really look as though it needed cutting, then I sat in his chair. Daddy said, 'Short back and sides.'

While I was having my hair cut, the barber next to me suddenly reached up and took a length of what looked like thin rope from a long bit that was hanging down from the ceiling and held it in a flame by the mirror and when it was alight he set fire to the hair of the man sitting in the next chair.

I've got this book at home called *Struwwelpeter* and it has this story about a boy who has his hair set on fire. There's another boy who has all his fingers cut off by someone with a pair of huge scissors and it used to keep me awake at night, and I thought for a moment it was going to happen to the man. When I asked Daddy afterwards why they did it, he said he had no idea, it was just one of the things they always did.

We went back to the office and Daddy made some telephone calls and kept going off and talking to people. It seemed pretty boring to me. I would hate to work in an office. I'm glad I'm going to be an actor when I grow up.

He finished work at about four o'clock and took me to Daniel Neal and bought me a new school cap.

We could have caught a train from Victoria and changed at

East Croydon, but Daddy wanted to travel home with his friends so we took a bus to London Bridge. They were all having a drink at the Bridge Hotel and I had to wait outside for a bit, but then they all came out and we went to get the 6.30. As we were getting into our compartment near the front, Dickie Pargeter called out to the engine driver, 'Don't forget to blow your whistle in Oxted tunnel and wake us, George,' and he didn't.

We got home at half-past seven. When Mummy asked me what I'd been up to all day, I told her most things, but I didn't mention anything about the game of bridge or seeing Uncle Bob. I told her the joke about Mrs Jones of Oxshott and she didn't get it either.

Thursday, January 17th

AFTER Daddy had gone to work, I was telling Mummy about them setting fire to the man's newspaper. I thought she'd laugh, but she sighed and said, 'The trouble with your father and his friends is that they think they're still in the army.'

When I asked her what she meant, she said, 'I don't know if you'll understand this, darling, but I'll say it anyway. When Daddy and his friends went off to war, they were really worried about what would happen to all of us. I expect they went on worrying for a while, but being hundreds of miles away, there was nothing they could do about it, so they stopped worrying and got on with fighting the Germans. They had no idea what it was like here, living through the bombs and the doodlebugs, and not having enough food and coal and clothes and petrol for nearly six years. They came home thinking life was going to carry on just as it had before. They didn't realise everything was damaged or worn out and that it was never going to be the same again. They're all finding it very hard to adjust to normal life, and they miss the excitement and the fun of Army life, so they try to keep it all going by meeting up in the pub all the time, or at the golf club, or on the train, and behaving as though they are still in the Officers' Mess, but they're not, and none of them seem to have realised it yet. That's what I meant. Anyway, I've got to get on and make the beds.'

I don't think she's as happy as she seems to be. Daddy and I have lots of jokes together and he is very jolly with his friends and they laugh a lot, but he and Mummy don't. They don't seem to talk to each other very much, either. It's not really surprising, I suppose, because they don't know each other very well. Not as well as Mummy and I know each other, anyway. We talk about lots of things together, but Daddy never really tells me much. He certainly never tells me how he's feeling, like Mummy does. And he still seems to go out all the time, especially at weekends, and he often comes home really late at night. He told me it was because he has a lot of work to do in the office, but he didn't seem to have that much to do when I was there.

I wish there was something I could do to make them happier, but I don't know what.

They've started a new adventure of Norman and Henry Bones, the boy detectives, on 'Children's Hour'. It's called 'The House in a Row', though when you look at it in the *Radio Times* it could be The House in a *Row* – like ours is sometimes. I'd really like to be like Norman and Henry and solve mysteries. If I was, I might be able to find out why Mummy said Uncle Bob had gone to South Africa when he hadn't, and why he gave me the canasta cards.

It's funny to think that Henry is played by Patricia Hayes who's a woman. You could never tell if you didn't know. She's very good, but I don't know why they don't have a boy. I think I'll write in to the BBC and ask if I can play the part.

Saturday, January 19th

THE snow's nearly all thawed now. There are a few grey patches here and there but the carrot and the pieces of coal in the middle of the lawn are all that are left of the snowman. It's really quite sad. But then Julian came round this morning and said did I want to go for a bike ride and then go back to his for lunch. I asked if it was going to be macaroni cheese and rabbit again, and he said no, they'd just had a food parcel from some relations in Canada and it included a tin of sausages and they were going to have those, so I said yes.

I was glad I went as the sausages were really tasty. They had also sent tea and sugar and chocolate and things, and after the sausages we had some chocolate blancmange made from the sugar and the chocolate. I never realised blancmange can actually taste quite nice. I wish we had relations in Canada.

Julian's parents didn't have lunch with us, but they came in afterwards and chatted to us. I really like them. Mrs Harrington asked me if I'd like to go up to London with them one day next week and see a show and have supper afterwards at the Hungaria. I said yes please, but I'd have to ask Mummy first. She said, 'I'll give her a ring.'

Colonel Harrington is still very thin, but he doesn't carry a stick any more. He doesn't talk anything like as much as Mrs Harrington. He said to me, 'Having a good holiday?' I said, 'Yes, thank you, sir.' He said, 'Good.' I asked him whether it was exciting being a Chindit. 'Damned uncomfortable,' he said. I said that Daddy had had an exciting time in the desert and that he had been a Desert Rat. Colonel Harrington frowned and said, 'Really?' I said yes and he'd known Monty really well. He said, 'Are you quite sure?' I said that's what he told me. The Colonel just grunted.

I wonder if I should have said anything. Perhaps it's all top secret still. How to find out, though, that's the thing. The more I think about it, the more I wish I was a boy detective.

Sunday, January 20th

JULIAN and I were on our bikes in a wood near Hurst Green when we discovered the ruins of an old house. All the windows had gone and the roof had fallen in. Julian said it was haunted and that a horrible crime had been committed in it which was why no one wanted to live there. When I asked him if it was true, he said, 'Who cares? It's bound to be more interesting than what really happened.' I said, 'You mean, like your father being in a Japanese prisoner-of-war camp?' He said, 'What do you mean? He *was* in one.' I said, 'But only for a few days. Not for months.' Julian shrugged and said, 'Who cares?' I said, 'But what you told me isn't true.' He said, 'Well, you told me your father was a Desert Rat.' I said, 'Well, he was.' Julian said, 'Are you sure?' I felt myself going really red and asked him what he meant. He said, 'Why don't you ask him yourself, if you don't believe me?' I said, 'Why should I?' He said, 'You can do what you like. I couldn't care less.'

I meant to say something to Daddy when I got home, but in the end I couldn't be fagged. I don't believe anything Julian says any more. In fact, I may not be friends with him next holidays.

Monday, January 21st

I WAS on my bike doing some skids on the icy bits outside Meadowcroft when I heard someone calling my name. I looked up and there, standing in one of the top windows, were Jill Pardoe and Amanda. They said did I want to come in, so I did. Jill said they'd just been out riding together on Limpsfield Common. Amanda asked me if I rode and when I said no, she said, 'You should. It's good fun and really easy. We've got a spare pony. You could come and ride him. I could teach you if you like.'

Jill giggled. When Amanda asked her what was so funny, Jill said, 'Amanda's a very good teacher, isn't she, Guy?' I said I didn't know what she meant. She said, 'Who taught you how to play Sardines?' and ran upstairs. Amanda pulled a face and said, 'It wasn't me, I didn't tell her,' and ran off after her. When the coast was clear, I slipped out of the back door and got on my bike and rode home.

Good riddance to bad rubbish, I say. I can't think why Amanda is friends with Jill in the first place. She's really stupid as far as I'm concerned. Jill, I mean. In fact, I've never really liked her. I was actually thinking of learning to ride, but I probably won't bother now.

Tuesday, January 22nd

WORMS was looking really fed up when he came in for his bread and cheese at elevenses. When I asked him what was the matter, he pulled out a copy of the *Daily Mirror* and pointed to a headline which said that the first of 50,000 English women who married American soldiers and airmen during the war are beginning to arrive at a special camp on their way to America to be reunited with their husbands. They're called GI Brides. According to this article, 344 of them have been taken to this place on a special train called

The Brides' Express, and 116 of them have children.

I asked Worms why he was fed up. He pointed to the last line of the article. It said the youngest bride was 16. I asked him if she was someone he knew. 'Only my Rosie,' he said. I said how could it be her, she's still at school.

'Was, you mean', he said. I said, was she married? 'As good as,' he said. When I asked what he meant, he said, 'She goes to stay with my sister in Lincolnshire for a couple of weeks last summer, right? She meets this Yank. He takes her for a drink – not that she's of an age, mind, but he doesn't know that and she doesn't say. Next thing she knows she's lying in a cornfield with her feet in the air and, Bob's your uncle, she's up the duff.'

I asked what the duff was. He said, 'She's going to have a baby.' I said how could she, she's only a little girl. He said, 'That's as may be, but she's a pregnant little girl now and she's on her way to America on the *Queen Mary* to marry this spotty Herbert of a Yank.' I said, 'Does she love him?' 'Love him?' said Worms. 'She's only met him the once.' I said I was really sorry. 'Yes, well,' said Worms, 'no use crying over spilt milk. I've got my seed potatoes to get sorted.' And he gulped down his tea and went outside and put his boots on.

I wonder if girls can get up the duff by kissing?

Wednesday, January 23rd

I'M going to have riding lessons at Captain Paget's riding stables on Limpsfield Common. Quite a few boys at school do it on Tuesday afternoons instead of rugger, including Gore-Andrews and Frobisher. Mummy's going to send me to school with a note tomorrow. I'm really looking forward to it. In fact, it's about the only thing I *am* looking forward to next term. I'm certainly not looking forward to having to wear Denis's cast-off shoes. They're really old and smell even worse than the socks and aertex shirts. I'm also worried about having to wear Mrs Pardoe's old jodhpurs.

Thursday, January 24th

DENIS'S shoes are even more uncomfortable than I'd imagined. He must have feet like a creature from outer space because there are lumps sticking up all over the place. Mummy says they'll wear down until they're the shape of my feet. I asked her if she meant some time this century. She said I worry too much. *She'd* worry if she had to go round all day with what feels like half of Pevensey Bay in her shoes.

Friday, January 25th

MISS Rump has left after only one term and we've got someone else for French called Mr Henbit. It's rather a good name for him as he looks as if he's been bitten by a hen. When I told Wetherby-Brown, he said he thought he looked as if he went round biting hens, more likely.

The Chimp came in before we had our first lesson with Mr Henbit and said we had to be very nice to him, as he had had rather a rough time of it in the war and had spent the last three years in a place called Colditz Castle. Apparently it was where they put the prisoners who kept trying to escape and it was easily the most uncomfortable prison camp in the whole of Germany and people who had been in it sometimes had difficulty adjusting to real life, so that if Mr Henbit behaved in a rather odd way from time to time we were to pretend we hadn't noticed.

It was impossible not to notice that he didn't know the difference between verbs that take *avoir* and verbs that take *être*, but we all pretended not to and didn't say anything whenever he got it wrong, which was every time.

He also had rather a peculiar accent and when Seabrook asked him why, he said it was because he had spent several months sharing a cell with some French prisoners from Marseilles. We asked him lots of questions about Colditz Castle and he told us all sorts of things, particularly about some prisoners who had tried to escape by building a glider and trying to fly out over the walls.

Wetherby-Brown said he wouldn't mind escaping from Badger's Mount and everyone said they wouldn't mind either. Mr Henbit said that, in that case, in our next French lesson he'd teach us how to build a glider like the one at Colditz, but that we weren't to breathe a word about it to anyone.

It was only after the bell had gone that we realised no one had asked him if the glider had worked.

Saturday, January 26th

DADDY went off to play golf with Mr Holmes-Johnson this afternoon. It's the first time he's played for years. While he was out, I said to Mummy, 'Daddy *was* a Desert Rat, wasn't he?' She said, 'He was in the desert, but I don't know if that automatically makes him a Desert Rat. Why don't you ask him?'

She made a vegetable pie for Sunday lunch and then said she had to pop out for a cup of tea with someone. When I asked who, she said I wouldn't know them.

I went down to Colin's and we got out his soap box. He and Rupert made it out of wooden packing cases and pram wheels and you steer it with a piece of rope attached to the bar at the front where you put your feet. We did time trials from the gate of his house to the bottom of the road. It gets really steep near the bottom and there's a sharp bend, almost a hairpin, where you have to lean out otherwise you can lose control and hit the bank on the far side. Unfortunately, I didn't lean far out enough on my third run and hit Major Freeman. Well, actually, I hit his walking stick and went all the way down to the bottom of the road with it lying across my lap. When I gave it back to him and said, 'I'm very sorry, Mr Freeman,' he said, 'It's Major Freeman, if you don't mind' in a really batey voice.

When I told Daddy later, he said, 'He has no right to call himself Major. He wasn't a regular. It was a First World War rank, and in point of fact he was only an acting major anyway. What do you suppose people would think if I went round calling myself Major Hodge?' I know what Anthony Masterson-Smith would think, and say.

Tuesday, January 29th

I HAD my first riding lesson today. I was outside the front door after lunch, waiting for the others, when The Chimp came out in his rugger kit and said, 'Well, Bodge, I hope you're better at riding than you are at rugger. The only tackle you'll have to face now is the saddle and bridle,' and ran off towards Lower Field.

I thought we were going to go on a bus or something, but we had to walk. It only took about half an hour so it wasn't too bad. The stables are next door to a cottage. There's one yard with four horse-boxes in it and then you go through a gate and down a path to another yard next to a field where there are four more boxes.

Captain Paget is a tall man with a red face who shouts a lot. 'You can ride Buttons,' he said. I thought from its name it would be a little fat pony, but it turned out to be a huge brown horse with a white patch on its forehead. I said, 'It's very big.' Captain Paget said, 'Fourteen hands and the gentlest horse in the stable. And for your information, it's a she.' I said, 'Does she go very fast?' He said, 'This isn't the Grand National, you know.'

One of the stable girls called Mary showed me how to put the saddle and bridle on and then it was time to mount. Captain Paget said, 'I'll give you a leg-up. Put your foot on here.' I thought he was pointing at something, but I couldn't see what. He said, 'Here, you bloody fool!' and I realised he wanted me to put my foot in his hand.

I didn't know it was possible to *be* so high off the ground. Every time the horse moved one of its feet I was sure I was going to fall off.

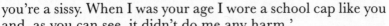

Most of the others were wearing riding hats so I asked Captain Paget if I could borrow one. He said, 'God, you're a sissy. When I was your age I wore a school cap like you and, as you can see, it didn't do me any harm.'

I quite enjoy riding, actually, but I felt a bit of a fool walking along on a leading rein with Mary while Gore-Andrews and Frobisher and people went galloping off with the Captain. When I told him I thought I'd got the hang of walking and could we trot, he said, 'Don't push your luck, chum.'

FEBRUARY

Friday, February 1st

WHEN Mr Henbit came in to take us for French this morning, he said, 'I hope you've all done your home-work.' Dishforth said, 'I have, sir,' and got up and put a sheet of paper on Mr Henbit's desk. Mr Henbit said, 'What the bloody hell's this meant to be, Dishcloth?' Dishforth said, 'It's my design for the glider, sir. What do you think?' Mr Henbit said, 'Glider? What the hell are you talking about?' Dishforth said, 'The glider for escaping from the school, sir.' Holmes-Johnson said, 'You know, sir, like the one you made in Colditz.' Then everyone started talking and reminding him what he said last week. He shouted, 'Shut up, the lot of you. Have you all gone stark raving mad? This is a French lesson. Now open your primers at page 23 – reflexive verbs ending in -re – and if I hear another word about gliders, you'll all be put in solitary. Is that clear?'

Saturday, February 2nd

THIS morning I helped Daddy do some digging in the vege-table garden. As we were cleaning the spades, I asked him what actual outfit he was with in the desert. He said, 'The Gunners. Royal Artillery. Why?' I said that I was telling Major Stanford-Dingley that my father had been in the desert like him and knew Monty and the Major had been really interested and wanted to know what lot he'd been with and I said I wasn't really sure, but I'd find out. Daddy said, 'Ah!' in an odd voice. I said, 'You do know Monty, don't you?' He said, 'Our paths crossed from time to time.'

Monday, February 4th

SAID the Cat to the Dog was on 'Children's Hour'. It's about this dog called Peckham, played by Stephen Jack, and this cat called Mompty, played by Vivienne Chatterton, and how they try to get on together.

Unfortunately, the programme only lasted twenty-five minutes and after that it was another boring Visit to Cowleaze Farm with Ralph Whitlock who talks very slowly, like a cow chewing grass. Colin says it's the way everyone talks in Devon and Cornwall where he goes on holiday. I'm quite glad I haven't been there if they're all as boring as the people in Cowleaze Farm.

Tuesday, February 5th

MY second riding lesson. I was allowed to trot for a while. I didn't realise you have to go up and down in your stirrups in time to the horse. It isn't as easy as it looks, especially not when Paget is telling me I look like a mixture between a sack of potatoes and a fat fairy on a blancmange. I don't think any of the others heard.

Wednesday, February 6th

IN table tennis this evening I beat Holmes-Johnson, who is the school champion, 21–12, 21–15, 21–18. I'm getting quite good, particularly with my forehand smashes.

Mr Henbit said he wouldn't mind a game and that he had been his school champion. Anyone can be champion of anything if they cheat as much as he does. Maths may not be my best subject, but I can count up to 21 and I know that 11 isn't followed by 13. Mr Henbit won the first game 21–19. I pretended I had some prep to do and asked if anyone else wanted to play in my place, but nobody did.

When I told Daddy, he said, 'Some people will go to any lengths to make themselves seem more important than they really are.'

Thursday, February 7th

MUMMY is really fed up because there's a food crisis in the world and the Germans are starving, so everyone's going to be really badly rationed. She said, 'Can you imagine? They're cutting butter and margarine from eight ounces a week to seven, and there won't be any more meat or eggs, and they're even cutting down on food for animals. It's worse than the war.'

I hope this doesn't mean the horses at Captain Paget's are going to go hungry. If so, I don't think I want to go riding again.

Friday, February 8th

BANANAS have arrived in Covent Garden market for the first time since before the war. Mummy said, 'And a fat lot of use they'll be.'

Saturday, February 9th

DADDY and I went down to Oxted on our bikes this morning to do the shopping and afterwards we popped in to Dickie Pargeter's. Dickie was just pouring him a Dry Fly when Daddy suddenly remembered he'd forgotten to buy any Camp coffee and left me while he went back to get some. I was having a small Tizer when Dickie said, 'Good chap, your old man. Salt of the earth. Follow him into the jungle any day.' I said I thought they were in the desert. He laughed and said, 'Figure of speech. Full marks for alertness, though.' I asked him if *he* was a Gunner, too. 'No fear,' he said. 'You wouldn't catch me sitting on my backside pooping off at Jerry two miles away. No, I was up there at the sharp end. Seventh Armoured Division. Desert Rats, they called us, after our divisional sign. Nasty thing called a jerboa. We adopted it on account of our scurrying and biting tactics in Libya.'

I said, 'So Daddy wasn't a Desert Rat, then?' Dickie said, 'Desert Tortoise, more likely.' He laughed. 'That's not to say he didn't do his bit. He did. We all did.'

I said, 'Do you think he might have met Monty?' Dickie said,

'Possible. Lot of people pressed the flesh at one time or another, including yours truly. Funny little man. Bloody good commander, though. More Tizer?'

Daddy came back soon after that and they both went out into the garden. On the way home Daddy said, 'You're very quiet. Everything okay?'

Sunday, February 10th

I was biking down the road on my way to see Colin after breakfast and was just passing Mr Henriksen's house when I happened to look up and there, standing in the bedroom window in a dressing gown, was Mrs Pardoe. I waved to her, but she didn't wave back. I suppose she must have stayed for the night, though I don't know why. She only lives a couple of doors away.

Monday, February 11th

Mummy bumped into Mrs Masterson-Smith this morning. She said that some new people have moved in next door to them in Robinswood Lane. The house is called Simla. A father and mother and two children, a boy and a girl. When Mummy said what was the matter with that, it's a very nice house, Mrs Harrington said, 'But they're cockneys. I'm sure they're very nice people in their own way, but can you imagine? In Robinswood Lane! And in Simla, of all houses!'

If Goering and Hess and Ribbentrop had moved in next door she could not have been in more of a state.

Tuesday, February 12th

I trotted again today. Captain Paget now calls me Potatoes all the time. It isn't very nice to be called that in front of the others, especially as Frobisher called me that at tea and now everyone's started doing it.

Wednesday, February 13th

THERE'S been a lot of rioting in India. It's because the Indians don't want to be ruled by the British any more, Daddy says. Yesterday a whole lot of people in Bombay set fire to banks and shops and the police came and opened fire and sixty people were killed. According to the *Daily Express*, a great storm is coming in India. Mummy is really worried about Aunt Rowena. Me too.

Thursday, February 14th

SOMEBODY has sent me a Valentine card. It has a heart with an arrow through it. Inside there's little poem which goes:

> My love is like a red, red rose
> That blooms in early spring.
> Who *is* my love, do you suppose?
> I durst not say a thing.

Instead of a signature there's a question mark, followed by a lot of crosses. The postmark says Sevenoaks which is where Amanda is at school. I felt really peculiar when I opened it and my heart was beating like it does after I've had a very hot bath. Mummy said, 'You're looking rather flushed. I hope you're not running a temperature.' I said I was fine, but actually I feel as if I'm about to explode at any moment. I have hidden the card in my *Radio Fun* Annual.

I couldn't help looking round at all the others in Form IV and wondering if they had had any Valentine cards. It didn't look like it. Anyway, they're all really ugly. I wouldn't want to send a card to any of them if I was a girl.

This afternoon the 1st XV was beaten 21–3 at home by Hazeldene and, as a punishment, the whole team was sent on an eight-mile run. I think on the whole I'd rather be called Potatoes than be in the 1st XV.

Friday, February 15th

In French today Mr Henbit told us that there are no words in the English language that end in one *l*. Dishforth said, 'How about "painful", sir?' Mr Henbit said, 'Are you trying to make me look a complete bloody fool?' Dishforth said, 'No, sir. It's just that there are quite a few words in English that end in one *l* and "painful" is one of them.' Mr Henbit shouted, 'Well, how about this for painful?' and he grabbed hold of Dishforth's hair and pulled him up out of his seat so hard that a great lump came out in his hand and the top of his head started bleeding and he had to go and see Matron.

Saturday, February 16th

Colin came round after lunch with a newspaper which said someone has invented an electronic brain. I've never seen him so excited. It's called an ENIAC which stands for Electronic Numerical Integrator and Computer. It has 18,000 electronic valves and no moving parts at all and it only takes seconds to work out sums and things that would take a human brain hours. Colin says it'll be ages before anyone will be able to buy one. I wish they'd hurry up so I could have one. Sums that take hours for human brains like Colin's to work out, take me days.

I said to Colin that perhaps one day someone might make an electronic brain that thinks. Colin said, they already have. It's called Mr Henbit. Unfortunately, all his wires have got crossed.

Mrs Masterson-Smith popped in this afternoon for a cup of tea. Their new neighbours in Simla are called Roberts. They haven't actually met them yet. They've seen them over the hedge and they don't look quite as bad as they'd first thought, but even so, she's told Anthony that if he happens to see them as he's passing he's to say 'Good morning' politely, but not to get into conversation. She said, 'We call him Bloody Roberts in our family. Not to his face, of course. That would be plain rude.'

Mummy said, 'Is it any wonder the Indians want us out of their country?'

Sunday, February 17th

THE Freemans next door in Bombers had a drinks party this morning. We were just getting ready to go up to the Pargeters, when Daddy came in and said we couldn't go because one of the Freemans' guests had parked their car across the top of our drive. Mummy said why didn't he go round and get them to move it? Daddy said, 'We have enough trouble with our neighbours as it is.'

We waited until people started leaving and then Daddy and I went out and hung about near the gate, pretending to do a bit of gardening. At last a large man with a red face and a big moustache came out of the Freemans' drive and went to the car and unlocked it. Daddy went out and said, 'Excuse me, but you've been blocking our entrance for the past hour.' The man said, 'Oh, really?' and opened the car door. Daddy said, 'We were supposed to visit some friends for a drink before lunch and thanks to you we have had to call it off.' The man said, 'Bad luck,' and started to get into his car. Daddy said, 'Frankly, I think you're extremely inconsiderate.' The man said, 'Do you really? And have you any idea who you're talking to?' Daddy said he didn't. The man said, 'I'm Colonel Anderson.' Daddy said, 'Well, I'm Brigadier Hodge.' The man jumped to attention and said, 'I'm most frightfully sorry, sir. Of course, had I known . . . I'll move the car straight away.' And he got in and drove off down the road.

Monday, February 18th

MR Henbit has left and Mr Reader is taking us for French until the new master arrives. Mr Reader knows less French than Mr Henbit and Miss Rump put together. When I whispered that to Wetherby-Brown, he whispered back that Mr Henbit and Miss Rump deserve to be put together and we nearly got the giggles. Mr Reader was really funny. He said he couldn't understand why English schoolchildren had to learn French at all. It's an ugly language spoken by ugly people with ugly characters, water that comes in bottles and sanitary arrangements that are older than the Ark. But since it's part of the Common Entrance syllabus, he supposed he'd better try and get some of it into our heads, and as long as he could keep one step ahead of us, there was an outside chance we might be able to stagger through it together.

Everyone cheered. I always used to think Mr Reader was a bit dull, but now I really like him.

Tuesday, February 19th

I'T'S been so cold the ground is frozen, so riding was cancelled.

Wednesday, February 20th

WE had a school lecture this evening, given by a deep-sea diver. It was the best one we've had since the time the man came with an eagle on his shoulder and asked for a volunteer and Seabrook went up and got pecked on the ear.

There were two really good bits this evening. One was when the diver came in in his diving suit and helmet. His lead boots were so heavy that the floor started shaking when he was still outside. Everybody laughed, but you could see that some of the junior boys were quite scared. We were all scared later when he showed us a stick of dynamite. He said that if he dropped it we would all be blown to kingdom come, and started throwing it up in the air and catching it. Then he pretended to drop it and caught it at the last minute. Some people screamed and Miss Longcroft almost fainted. The diver laughed and said he *did* drop a stick of dynamite at one school and the first person down was the headmaster. We all looked at The Chimp to see if he was laughing. He was, but you could tell he was quite worried, though not as worried as we were.

Thursday, February 21st

I WAS cycling home over the Common this afternoon and saw this man and woman walking along in the distance holding hands and for a moment thought it was Mummy and Uncle Bob. I got quite a shock. But, of course, I soon realised it couldn't have been them because when I got home a few minutes later, Mummy was in the kitchen listening to someone on the wireless giving a recipe for squirrel pie. I hope she's not thinking of cooking it for us.

Friday, February 22nd

A BOY in Form II called Ham was caught during Break climbing Big Oak which is out of bounds. The Chimp came out and told him to come down straight away and go to his study. Ham said, 'Please, sir, are you going to beat me?' The Chimp said, 'Don't be ridiculous, Ham, of course I'm going to beat you.' Ham started to blub and said, 'Please, sir, I don't want to be beaten.' The Chimp said, 'I don't want you to climb Big Oak, Ham, but you did anyway.' Ham started blubbing even more and said, 'Please don't beat me, sir. If you do, my father will beat me as well.' The Chimp said, 'What your father does or doesn't do is none of my concern, now come down at once.' But Ham refused, so The Chimp said he'd have to stay up there until he saw sense. He didn't see sense and stayed up there for the rest of the morning.

We all tried to persuade him to come down and said that six of the best was better than being frozen to death, but he refused to move. I could see him out of the window from my desk all through Double Maths and felt really sorry for him. It was freezing cold and he was only wearing a pullover, and the scars on his knees were bright blue. In the end his mother had to come and take him away. The Chimp came in during lunch and gave us a pi-jaw about courage and facing up to responsibilities and said that in twenty years of teaching he had never come across such moral feebleness as Ham had shown and he hoped that would be a lesson to us all. By the time he'd finished, all our spotted dicks were cold, but we were made to eat them anyway.

Daddy said he would be home in time for supper followed by the Army edition of 'Merry-Go-Round' in Studio Stand Easy. Personally I don't think it's as funny as the Air Force edition at Much-Binding-In-The Marsh or the Navy edition in HMS *Waterlogged* at Sinking-in-the-Ooze, but I quite like Sergeant 'Cheerful' Charlie Chester and the happy band of 'Other Cranks' from 'Stars in Battledress', and although I think Will Hay's films are boring, he's quite funny when he does the Service Double-or-Quits Cash Quiz. The questions are really easy, though. I don't know why Daddy doesn't go in for it and get some money so we can go on holiday next summer at Angmering-on-Sea, like Amanda and her parents do.

I was going to ask him this evening, but he didn't come home in time after all. He did while I was having my bath, but when I called out to him to come up, he sounded really peculiar. His voice was all slurred and he said he was going to get something to eat first. I heard him go into the kitchen and there was a terrific crash and a lot of shouting. I wanted to get out of the bath and see if he was all right, but Mummy said she'd go, and she went down and there was a lot more shouting, and then I heard someone go into the hall and the front door slammed and then there was a long silence and I got out and dried myself and got into bed and ages later Mummy came in. I could see she had been crying, and when she came to kiss me goodnight I asked her what the matter was and she burst into tears and said it didn't matter, it was nothing to do with me, and rushed out of the room.

I was quite sorry when the war first ended, but I'm even sorrier now.

Saturday, February 23rd

DADDY seemed to be the same as usual this morning. He didn't say anything about last night and I didn't either. The only thing that was different today was that we didn't pop up to the Pargeters' after shopping. When I asked him why, he said, 'No reason,' and didn't say anything for the rest of the morning.

We didn't talk much during lunch and I was quite pleased

when Colin came round and I could get down and we went to his house and mucked about. Rupert has bought an old Douglas motorbike and we stood around while he tinkered with the engine and then he gave us rides on it round the garden. The clutch was very sharp and the back wheel made terrible marks in the lawn, but nobody seemed to mind. As long as he doesn't suggest trying it out on our lawn.

We got rather bored after a bit and Colin said why didn't we go to the four o'clock matinee at the Plaza? We looked in the *Surrey Mirror* to see what was on. I thought it was going to be *The Bandit of Sherwood Forest* which they were talking about in Going to the Pictures in 'Children's Hour' the other day, but that's not till next week. This week it's something called *Brief Encounter* which is an A-film and ended on Wednesday anyway, and from Thursday to Saturday it's a U-film called *I Know Where I'm Going*. It said it was about a girl who goes to a Scottish island to marry someone and gets into a whirlpool and is rescued by another man who takes her to another island and she falls in love with him and they live happily ever after.

I said it sounded a bit girly to me, but Colin said it was either that or mucking about, so I went to ask Daddy and he said okay but come straight home and we bicycled down and went into the shilling seats. Luckily, there was a Mr Pastry film on first which was really funny and the 'Topical Budget' was about the riots in India which are much worse than I thought, and how there's only one week's supply of coal left in the whole of London.

The back row was full, so we had to sit in the one in front. Luckily the next row down was empty, so we were able to dangle our feet over the back of the seats. Just before the film started, we went to the lavatory and got back to find a couple sitting slap in front of us, so we had to sit up properly.

Actually, the film wasn't as bad as I thought it would be. The whirlpool bit was quite exciting, but I couldn't concentrate properly because the couple in front kept moving their heads,

so we had to keep moving our heads as well in order to see past them. After a while the woman rested her head on the man's shoulder. Colin and I both got the giggles. Then the man turned his head and kissed her. We tried to stop giggling by holding our noses, but it made things even worse. Suddenly the man turned round and said, 'Why don't you two little squirts buzz off and leave us in peace?'

At that moment the screen went bright and I suddenly saw it was Uncle Bob. When he saw it was me, he said, 'Oh, my God!' and then the woman turned and I saw it was Mummy.

I remember her saying, 'It's all right, darling, I can explain,' something like that, and then next thing I knew I was running out of the cinema and jumping onto my bike and pedalling as fast as I could go up Hoskins Road. I don't know what Colin was doing. I didn't really care. All I know is that I wanted to get as far away from the cinema as I could.

I cycled round for ages and ages, I don't know where exactly. Then I went to Anthony's and stayed there for a long time. Luckily, his parents were out so I didn't have to explain anything. It was pitch dark and freezing cold when I got home. Mummy and Daddy must have heard me putting my bike away because they both came out to find me. Mummy was crying and putting her arms round me and saying how worried they had been and how sorry she was and she could explain everything, it wasn't what it looked like, and Daddy stood there, smoking his pipe and frowning, but not saying anything.

I didn't want to talk about it and said I wanted to go to bed. Mummy said would I like some soup, but I didn't feel like anything. She didn't say anything when she came in to see if I was in bed, except 'I'm so sorry, darling.'

I'm writing this in bed. There are lots of things I want to say, but I can't think how to say them. It's a bit like writing an essay for Mr Reader. I think I'll stop now and go to sleep. Perhaps everything will be better in the morning.

Sunday, February 24th

I WOKE up very early and couldn't go back to sleep, so I got up to go downstairs and saw that Mummy and Daddy's door was open. I went in, but there was no one there. I went downstairs and Mummy was sitting at the table in the morning room in a dressing-gown with a cup of tea, hugging herself as if she was very cold. I asked where Daddy was and she said he'd gone to Dickie Pargeter's. I said it was a bit early for sherry. She said, 'Actually, he went last night.' When I asked where he was now, she said she expected he was still there. I said I didn't understand and she said she didn't either, but she and Daddy had had an argument and he had decided to go and stay with the Pargeters. I asked when he was coming back and she said she didn't know, it was all her fault. She should have told Uncle Bob she couldn't see him any more when Daddy came home and made him go to South Africa, as he promised, and she would never have seen him again.

I asked her if she loved Uncle Bob and she said yes, but not in the same way she loved Daddy, or me. I asked her if she meant she just liked kissing him a lot and she said, 'Sort of.' She said she just wanted to see him all the time, she couldn't really explain why, she just did. She said she didn't expect me to understand, but I do actually. It's like me and Amanda. I really love kissing her and everything, but I don't love her in the same way that I love Mummy. When I told her that, she laughed and said, 'If only it was that simple.' Of course, it isn't quite the same thing because I'm not married to Mummy, but it's true anyway. I do want to see Amanda all the time – well, not *all* the time, not when I'm mucking about on Colin's brother's motorbike, or reading *Radio Fun*, or going on a bike ride with Julian, but most of the rest of the time – and I definitely wouldn't try and get her to go to South Africa.

Anyway, whatever Mummy says, I still think it might be my fault. If I hadn't been here when Daddy came back from the war, he and Mummy might have got on much better and she wouldn't have wanted to see Uncle Bob again, and he would have gone to South Africa after all, and I wouldn't have seen them kissing in the cinema, and Daddy would be living here instead of at the Pargeters'.

Anyway, I don't feel like writing any more today.

Monday, February 25th

A CCORDING to the *Daily Express*, a little girl has died from eating too many bananas. If we had any bananas, I'd eat the whole lot.

Mummy went up the road to see Mrs Pardoe about something after tea, so instead of listening to 'Children's Hour', I went into Mummy's bedroom and started looking through their things. I found a cardboard box on top of the wardrobe and when I opened it, there was a revolver inside in a leather holster. It had a WD sign stamped onto it, so I knew it must have been the one Daddy had in the Army. I wondered how many people had been killed with it and whether he'd ever killed any Germans. There were no bullets in the box, so I took it out to the shed and got the bullet I'd found in Staffhurst Road out of my saddlebag. I tried to fit it into one of the holes in the revolver, but it was much too big, so I put it back in the saddlebag and put the revolver back into the box and put it back on top of the wardrobe and went and did my History homework.

I really don't want to go riding tomorrow, but I'm looking forward to seeing Buttons again. At least animals don't let you down like people do.

* * *

APRIL

Friday, April 12th

IT is six weeks and four days since I had my accident. I have been meaning to start my journal again, and I have often sat down and picked up my pen, but I couldn't be fagged to write anything down. I keep trying to remember what happened, but I can't. Mummy says I'm probably still suffering from the effects of concussion. I remember it was very cold and icy and I skidded once or twice on the way to school. In Break The Chimp told us riding had been cancelled. I was pretty fed up, not just because this was the second time running, but because the rugger pitches were all frozen, so instead of games, everybody was going to have to go on a six-mile run, including the riders.

But then the sun came out just before lunch and Captain Paget rang up to say it was a shame to waste such a beautiful day and that we were going for a short ride in the Chart Woods after all.

It all started off all right, and Buttons seemed really pleased to see me. She was a bit friskier than usual, but Mary said it was only high spirits and she was excited at going out for the first time for ages. The Captain shouted out that no one was allowed to canter and that we could only trot when he said so. I said did I have to be on the leading rein and he said it was better to be safe than sorry.

It was really nice in the woods. The silver birches looked white against the blue sky, like a photograph of New England I once saw in a *National Geographic* magazine in the dentist's waiting-room. It was pretty cold, but luckily I'd remembered to wear an extra pullover under my school blazer and to put on my school scarf, and my school cap is quite warm when it's pulled right down.

Everything was going all right and we were just coming to a place where the path crossed another, when suddenly a bird flew up beside me and the next thing I knew I was galloping down this path with the leading rein flapping behind me. I tried to pull on the reins to make Buttons stop, but I couldn't and, anyway, I was too busy trying to stay on and the branches were slashing me in the face and my cap came off and I didn't know what to do. I shouted for help, but I must have been a long way away by then and I don't suppose anybody could hear me.

I remember being really worried in case I met someone coming the other way, some children on bicycles, perhaps, or a mother pushing a pram. The path was getting narrower and narrower and I didn't know how I was going to get out of the way.

And then suddenly I came to the end of the path and found myself galloping across the playground of the local school. The ground was completely frozen and we were going straight towards some goal-posts, and I suddenly realised that if we went under them I would be knocked off by the crossbar and probably killed.

I once saw a Roy Rogers film where he was galloping towards a low branch and, as he went under, he grabbed the branch and held on and Trigger went galloping on and Roy was left swinging on the branch. I was wondering if that's something you can do in real life, and the next thing I knew I was lying in bed in this very white room and Daddy was standing there with a nurse and Mummy was sitting at the side of the bed holding my hand and asking if I was all right.

I don't remember saying anything, but I must have done because they all smiled and then Mummy cried and Daddy said, 'We're here, old chap, everything's going to be all right', and then I must have gone back to sleep because the next thing I knew it was dark except for this tiny lamp and I heard

Mummy saying, 'It's all right, darling, you've had a nasty bang on the head, try not to move', and then it was light again and my head hurt and I put my hand up and felt this huge bandage, and the nurse came in and took my temperature and asked if I was hungry and I said yes, could I have some bananas, and she laughed and went out, and the next thing I knew, Mummy and Daddy were there again and Daddy was saying, 'Well, you certainly gave us a fright and no mistake.'

It was all very muddling, and I had lots of strange dreams with peculiar creatures in them I've never seen before, and I kept waking up and sometimes it was light and sometimes it was dark and sometimes Mummy and Daddy were there and sometimes the nurse and sometimes no one. It was really peculiar.

When I felt better and was able to sit up, Mummy told me I had been completely unconscious for three days and half-conscious for another three and that it had been touch and go whether they'd have to operate or not.

A doctor kept coming in and asking me if I could remember what had happened just before the accident, but I couldn't. He said it didn't matter and that it would probably come back to me eventually, but it still hasn't, actually.

Mummy and Daddy told me that Buttons must have slipped on the ice and fallen just before she got to the goal-posts and then got up and galloped off down the road. When Captain Paget and the others finally got there, I was still lying on the ground in a pool of blood. According to Gore-Andrews and Frobisher, Mary burst into tears and Captain Paget said, 'For God's sake, girl, he's not dead. Stop blubbing and do something.' Apparently he never even got off his horse to look.

Mummy says that Dickie Pargeter told Daddy that Captain Paget is obviously a crook and he ought to take him to court and get lots of money out of him, but Daddy says it's better to let sleeping dogs lie. Dickie said that dogs like Captain Paget should be whipped and thrown off the Viaduct and that he would be only too happy to do it himself.

I had to stay in hospital for ages. Actually, it was really good fun. I was in the Men's Ward and Mr Worthington in the next bed, who works for the Gas Board and looks like Harold Berens in 'When Ignorance is Bliss', made me laugh every time he opened his mouth. Whenever the man in the bed at the far end who'd had a stroke used to let off, Mr Worthington would go round sprinkling the place with talcum powder. Everyone complained that the talcum powder smelt worse than the let-off, and the moment he started we all hid under our bedclothes, but he used to do it anyway.

Once we were all listening in to 'Those Were the Days' with Harry Davidson on our earphones when Mr Worthington hopped out of bed, grabbed Sister Grice and started doing a Military Two-Step with her. I laughed so much I thought I was going to be sick and very nearly was. And then, right in the middle of it, somebody shouted 'Grice!' and we all looked round and there was Matron standing in the doorway, and we all had to hide under the bedclothes because we were laughing so much, and Mr Worthington was sent back to bed and told he wasn't to get out again for the rest of the day. When he asked what about going to the lavatory, Matron said, 'It's bedpans and bottles for you, Mr Worthington.' You often hear about people dying laughing. I always thought it was just a thing people said, but now I think it could really happen.

'Those Were the Days' used to be one of my worst programmes, but now every time I hear it, it makes me burst out laughing. I still hate 'Grand Hotel' with Albert Sadler and his Orchestra, though.

The other good thing about being in hospital was that I was able to have a boiled egg every day. I don't know where Mummy got them from, but she brought them in every week in a box and each one had my name written on it in pencil. Colin came to see me and brought me the latest *Radio Fun*, which was really good. I usually hate Arthur Askey. He's called The Little Man with the Big Heart. The Little Man with the Big Head would be a better description. He's always rushing around with a silly hat on his face and a stupid grin on his head – the other way round, I mean – and calling everyone 'playmate' and saying 'ta, everso', but this time even he was actually quite amusing. Everybody wanted to read it and Mr Worthington did one of the best imitations of Colonel Chinstrap I've ever heard. Sister Grice did one of Ethel Revnell which was even worse than the real thing.

Lots of other people came to see me as well, including Mrs

Phipps and The Chimp, who said, 'Ten out of ten for moral fibre,' and Mr Reader, who told me a joke which went 'The man turned on his heel and the damned fool forgot to turn it off again' and lent me one of his bound copies of *Strand* magazines which had some really good Sherlock Holmes stories in it with pictures – 'The Five Orange Pips', 'The Musgrave Ritual', 'The Lion's Mane' and 'The Solitary Cyclist' – plus some W. W. Jacobs stories about bargemen on the Thames, which I quite enjoyed but not as much as the Sherlock Holmes. Actually, Mr Reader looks a bit like I imagine Sherlock Holmes looked. I really like him now.

One day Mrs Pardoe came with Jill and Tessa and brought a bunch of grapes. I've never had grapes before. They were rather sour, and everyone else in the ward wanted to have one, so there were hardly any left for me in the end, which was just as well.

Tessa was rather silly, as usual, and kept giggling for no reason, but Jill was quite nice for a change and asked me about the accident and everything. She said, 'I bet you only did riding because Amanda does.' I said actually it was because I wanted to get out of rugger. I said, not sounding as if I cared, that I wondered if Amanda would be coming to see me at half-term. Jill said she'd ask her, but she didn't think so, and when I asked her why, Tessa giggled and said, 'Didn't you know? She's gone on Andrew Henderson.' Jill said, 'Shut up, Tessa.' I said, 'I couldn't care less', and felt myself going red, which was really annoying. Luckily I didn't cry, but I jolly nearly did.

After they'd gone, Mr Worthington said, ''Ullo, 'ullo. *Cherchez la femme!*', which made me laugh. I don't know what it means exactly, but it made me feel much better anyway.

Actually, I never liked Amanda that much anyway. I just liked kissing her, that's all. I thought she liked kissing me, but you can never tell with girls.

After two weeks in hospital they discovered I'd cracked a bone in my back, and instead of going back to school I had to spend another three weeks at home lying on a bed in the morning room with a pillow under my back and nothing under my head and not being allowed to move. It was incredibly boring and I felt really homesick for the hospital and Mr Worthington and his jokes and all the friends I'd made in the ward. I even missed the man with the stroke letting off.

Lots of my friends came to see me, including Wetherby-

Brown, Briggs, Holmes-Johnson, Seabrook and Frobisher, and told me what was happening at school, which sounded pretty boring except for when Gilbert got six for biting Vole's ear during the House Boxing Competition, and someone in Form III let Major Stanford-Dingley's pigs out by mistake and they all ran off down the road to Crockham Hill, and even though it was dark and pouring with rain, the whole of the form were told to go off and not come back until they'd caught every single one.

I also missed the 'Varsity Boat Race. Mummy brought the wireless through and we listened to it together, but it wasn't the same as sitting in the dining hall at school and following it on the map of the river that The Chimp draws every year on a blackboard and we all shout for Oxford or Cambridge and as the boats reach different points along the course like Craven Steps and Chiswick Eyot and Duke's Meadows, The Chimp draws them on the board to show where they are.

Oxford won, which was a pity as I support Cambridge myself, partly because of Daddy but also because I like light blue better than dark blue.

In the end I was allowed to go back to school on Thursday, April 4th, which wasn't much good as it was the end of term the following Wednesday and, anyway, I wasn't allowed to muck about or anything, though when it was games I had to go down and watch.

Anyway, now it's the holidays again, and I'm not allowed to go out on my bike for the first week, so that's why I've decided to start my journal again. The trouble is, there's not very much to write about. Julian's not home yet and the Penwardens have gone to Cornwall. Still, at least Daddy came back, on Mummy's birthday actually, and they don't seem to have rows any more like they used to and she doesn't drink anything like as much gin as she did. She still smokes quite a lot, though.

Neither of them said anything about it and I didn't either, except I did ask Mummy one day if Uncle Bob knew about my accident and she said, 'I wouldn't know. He's in South America.' I said, 'Don't you mean South Africa?' She said, 'No, South America.' I said, 'Honestly?' 'Honestly,' she said. 'Cross your heart and hope to die?' 'The first part, anyway,' she said, and kissed me on the forehead.

Monday, April 15th

MY school report arrived this morning. Most of them said how sorry they were that I'd missed most of the term and The Chimp said I had a lot of catching-up to do if I wanted to acquit myself creditably in Common Entrance next term. He also said, 'He is obviously not a boy who accepts a setback. Just the right spirit, this. Well done, Guy!'

Major Stanford-Dingley seems to be the only one who hasn't heard about my accident and doesn't seem to realise I've been away. He wrote, 'I wish he'd show more life on the rugger field. I'm tired of seeing him standing on the touchline in his overcoat – though it is a very nice overcoat.'

Thursday, April 18th

TODAY we went to look round Farnleigh which is where my parents want me to go next. It's in Surrey somewhere. Daddy was there and says it's the best school in England. I said, what about Eton? and he said, apart from Eton, and I said, what about Winchester? and he said, *and* Winchester, and I said, what about Harrow? and he said, anything's better than Harrow.

Actually, some of my friends are going to Harrow, and Julian's going to Eton. No one I know is going to Farnleigh. Daddy said that's a good thing, it's time I made some new friends. I like the friends I've got now.

The master that took us round kept pointing out places with funny names like Underwood's Passage and Harrison's Halfpenny, and explaining that the new boys are called Runts, and have to runt, or fag, for the senior boys who are called Bulls and are allowed to carry canes and beat Runts without permission from the Head Magister.

There's a book of school rules, customs and slang called 'The Farnleigh Four Hundred' which is called that because it contains four hundred rules, customs and slang words and every Runt has to learn them all by heart, and after a month he has to stand on a table without any clothes on, balancing a glass of bathwater on his head, and be tested by the most senior boys of all who are called Bull's Bloods, and if he makes a single bish or tips over the glass, he has to drink the contents.

The master and Daddy, who'd been at Farnleigh together (in fact the master runted for Daddy for the whole of his first year), swapped yarns about things that had happened in their day and roared with laughter. I said I thought it sounded horrible and they laughed all the more and said it never did them any harm, and that they counted themselves lucky to have gone to a school that treasured its customs and hadn't let standards slip as so many other schools were doing now the war was over.

When the master said did I have any comments to make, I said Farnleigh must be a very old school. He said, 'Older than some and not as old as others.' When I asked him how old, he said, 'We were given our charter by Prince Henry in '21.' I said, '1521?' He said, 'No, 1921.'

I always thought Daddy went to one of the oldest public schools in England. I suppose it doesn't matter really, but I'm not really looking forward to going there very much. Perhaps if I fail my Common Entrance I won't have to. The way things are going, I stand a very good chance.

Saturday, April 20th

MUMMY has organised for me and Julian and Jill Pardoe to join a ballroom dancing class at the Hoskins' Arms Hotel, starting on Monday. I can't imagine anything worse – except being a Runt at Farnleigh.

Monday, April 22nd

MY first dancing lesson. Julian and Jill and I went down together on our bikes. When we got there, we found lots of people we knew, like Anthony Masterson-Smith and Barbara Kippax and the Urquarts and Holmes-Johnson, who was looking really embarrassed. He came up to me and whispered, 'You won't say anything about this to anyone at school, will you?' 'Of course not, Holmes-Johnson,' I said. 'Do you promise?' he said. 'I promise,' I said, crossing both toes.

The lady who runs the dancing classes is called Miss du Fray. She comes from Woldingham and has a white poodle called Antoine and a French accent. She said, 'I am really

Mademoiselle du Fray and you should call me Mademoiselle, as the girls in my school in Paris did before the war when I taught them ballet and how to curtsey, etcetera, but *malheureusement*, things are not what they were and now I must be satisfied with the quickstep and the rumba and plain Miss. Ah well, *tant pis*.' Her accent was even worse than Miss Rump's, in my opinion.

We spent the whole of the first hour just walking up and down in a line in time to Roy Fox playing 'Making Whoopee' on a wind-up gramophone. Then we learnt how to step to the *gauche* and the *droite*. Then we learnt how to do a sort of shuffle. It looked quite easy when Miss du Fray did it, but none of us could, so she said, 'Antoine and I will show you,' and she went across and lifted the poodle onto its back legs and made it do the steps with her.

Julian said, 'I know there's a shortage of men at dances these days, but surely this is going too far.' Miss du Fray said, 'Perhaps you would care to demonstrate, since you seem to be such an expert?' Julian said, 'No, thank you, mademoiselle. I wouldn't want to tread on your toes.' Afterwards I said to Jill, 'I think Julian's quite funny, don't you?' She said, 'Quite.'

Monday, April 29th

Second dancing lesson. We did some more walking up and down and Miss du Fray demonstrated some more steps with Antoine and we practised those – though it's a bit difficult trying to copy a poodle.

Then we had a break for orange squash and Marie biscuits and then Miss du Fray said, 'Now, take your partners!'

Everyone was wandering around, trying to decide who to choose, when suddenly Jill came rushing across from the other side of the room and said, 'Will you dance with me?' I was quite surprised as I thought she would have preferred someone like Julian, but I said yes anyway.

There's an expression I've heard about people being made for each other, and Jill and I are definitely made for each other when we do the quickstep. We never tread on each other's toes, or turn the wrong way, or anything. Jill said, 'You're a much better dancer than Antoine.' I said, 'Do you really think so?' She said, '*You're* funny.'

After we had practised for a bit, we all had to do a little demonstration in front of the rest. The prize for the best couple was a packet of sweet cigarettes. I thought we were easily the best, especially as Anthony and Lettice tripped over, and Julian and Barbara Kippax did it holding each other the wrong way round. When we finished, Miss du Fray said, 'Very good, but I can tell that you two have danced together before.' When we said we hadn't, she said, 'You are very naughty children, I know you have,' and gave the prize to Anthony and Lettice.

Afterwards I told Jill I thought it was really unfair. She said, 'Never mind, would you like to come home and have some lemonade?' I said, 'What about Julian?' She said, 'What about him?'

There was nobody at Meadowcroft when we got there. We had some lemonade, and Jill said, 'Shall we go into the garden?' I said I didn't mind, so she went out and I followed. We walked down to the end and sat on the diving board by the swimming pool and talked about the dancing class. Then we went in and had some more lemonade and went back down to the pool and sat there. After a while she said, 'Do you still like Amanda?' I said, 'Not really.' She said, 'I think the only reason you liked her in the first place was because she kissed you.' I said, 'Maybe.' She said, 'Would you like to kiss me?' I said, 'Maybe.' She said, 'You can if you like.' So I did.

She wasn't anything like as good at kissing as Amanda, but I don't expect she has had as much practice. It wasn't too bad, all the same.

We stopped kissing and then I said, 'Shall we do it again?' and she said, 'I don't mind', so we did it again.

Suddenly Jill's mother appeared from nowhere and shouted, 'What do you think you're doing?'

We both jumped up. I said, 'Nothing, Mrs Pardoe.' Jill said, 'We weren't doing anything wrong, honestly.'

Mrs Pardoe said, 'I've been watching you both for the last ten minutes and I don't need to be told what's right and what's wrong, thank you very much. May I remind you that Jill is barely thirteen.'

I said, 'But I'm only thirteen too. I will be on Wednesday week, anyway.'

Mrs Pardoe said, 'Well, you should know better. Jill, go to your room at once. As for you, you can get out of my garden and don't come back here again. I'll be speaking to your mother about this shortly.'

I didn't know what to say, so I just ran as fast as I could down to the very bottom of the garden and through the woods and back into our garden.

There was nobody at home, so I went upstairs to my room and sat on my bed. It felt really odd being suddenly there, especially as I didn't know what it was that I'd done wrong.

When Mummy came back at lunchtime, she found me lying on my bed and asked me if I was all right. I didn't want to tell her what had happened, but I did anyway.

She said, 'Right, I'm going to sort this out straight away,' and she went downstairs and I heard the front door slam and her footsteps crunching on gravel in the drive.

She was away for ages, and when she came back, she said, 'I think it would be best for everyone's sake if you and Jill didn't see each other until next holidays. By then perhaps everything will have been forgiven and forgotten.'

I said, 'But we didn't do anything wrong.' She said, 'I'm sure you didn't.' I said, 'We were only having a little kiss.' She said, 'I know.' I said, 'Anthony Masterson-Smith once asked Lettice Urquart to pull her knickers down.' Mummy said, 'Well, as long as you don't.' I said, 'I don't understand. Mrs Pardoe kisses other people, so why does she get het up when other people do?' Mummy said, 'I don't know, and I don't expect she does either.'

The trouble is, I really like Jill now and I don't think I can wait until next holidays. That's not for another three months and she might easily meet someone else in the meantime, like Amanda did. I don't know what to do.

MAY

Wednesday, May 1st

A REALLY boring day with nothing to do. I was listening to a programme called 'A Visit to Pinewood' and suddenly realised what a lot of stations you can get on your wireless if you want. I know where some of the places are, like Toulouse and Lille and Oslo and Reykjavik, but some I've never heard of. Where on earth is Softens, and Hilversum, and Allouis, and Tromso? And why would anyone want to tune in to any of them? Who cares? As long as we don't have to.

Sunday, May 5th

I HAVE been up to Meadowcroft every day for the last week and waited behind the hedge hoping Jill might come out, but she never has.

I suppose I could write to her at school. The trouble is, I've never written to a girl before, so I don't quite know what to say.

Monday, May 6th

I GOT a letter this morning. It said NOT TO BE OPENED TILL MAY 8TH. I took it up to my room and opened it anyway. It was a birthday card from Jill. She said she was really sorry, she really liked me and she wanted to see me to explain, but she'd had to go back to school on May 1st and she hoped I'd write to her. I definitely will now.

Tuesday, May 7th

I⊤'s my thirteenth birthday tomorrow. I can't believe it's a year since Hitler committed suicide and the war came to an end. According to Mrs Phipps, he took poison *and* shot himself. I think I might do the same if I pass Common Entrance and have to go to Farnleigh.

It's been another really boring day. Julian's gone back to school and Colin has had to go to the dentist's in Redhill. I listened to Rex Alston commentating on the third day of India *v.* Worcestershire, but that was pretty boring too, so because there wasn't anything else to do, I went up to Anthony's and we mucked about on our bikes. It was okay.

We were coming back down Robinswood Lane without hands when we saw this girl leaning over the gate at Simla. She called out, 'Hallo, Anthony, would you like to go for a bike ride one day?'

Anthony went like a Belisha beacon and said 'Good afternoon' and pedalled off up the road at high speed.

She said, 'How about you, then?' I got off and went across and started chatting to her. Her name's Rita. She's thirteen and a bit and very nice to talk to and makes lots of jokes and knows quite a lot about cricket. After a while you hardly notice she's a cockney at all. Also, she's quite pretty. She looks a bit like Dorothy Lamour, actually, but much younger, of course. I might easily go for a bike ride with her one day. It depends.